MURDER
at
PELICAN LAKE

Marjorie Mathison Hance

ISBN 13: 9798354068241
Library of Congress Catalog Number: 2018907150
Printed in the United States of America
Second Printing: 2019
23 22 21 20 19   6 5 4 3 2

Cover art: Illustration © Marcella Rose. All rights reserved.
www.marcellarose.com
Book design and typesetting by Dan Pitts.

North Lakes Press,
10985 - 56th Avenue North, Plymouth, MN 55442
(952) 484-2824
northlakespress@gmail.com

To order: Individual copies are available through Amazon.com or www.northlakesmurdermysteries.com. Bulk order discounts are available through North Lakes Press.

Contact Marjorie Mathison Hance at mmhance4@gmail.com for speaking engagements, book club discussions, freelance writing projects, and interviews.

Murder at Pelican Lake is the first book in the North Lakes Murder Mystery Series. Book Two, *Cormorant in the Net*, and Book Three, *The Man Three Cottages Down*, are also available on Amazon or through www.northlakesmurdermysteries.com.

PROLOGUE

Monday

The girls chattered and laughed as they strolled down the street. The bright blue sky was a contrast to the disappearing orange school bus. Friends since kindergarten, the three lived only a few blocks from each other in Vergas, Minnesota, and now were sophomores at the high school in Frazee, about eight miles away. One of the girls playfully shoved the other.

"You like him, you like him."

"Shut up."

"Lindsey and Paul sitting in a tree. K-I-S-S-I-N-G. First comes—"

"Very funny. You're one to talk," Lindsey taunted back.

"Everybody knows I like Jonathan. Except Jonathan. I've had a crush on him since fourth grade. Unrequited love." Eleanor sighed. "Too bad it's the end of the school year. You won't see Paul again until next fall."

"Why not?"

"Because he lives with his dad in the Cities over the summer."

"How did you find that out?"

"Because, unlike you, I talk to him. Yes, talk to him. In person. Actually, I wanted to find out if he likes you. So, I asked him." Eleanor

paused for dramatic effect. "He does," she announced with an air of authority.

Lindsey blushed and felt her heart skip a beat. She liked him too. They were friends on Facebook, but that was about the extent of their interaction.

As they approached Long Lake, the three friends waved good-bye. Eleanor and Michelle lived on the same block and turned left to go home, while Lindsey continued along the street bordering the lake.

Tomorrow night, they'd have a sleepover at Michelle's to celebrate the start of summer vacation. The three were so in sync with one another everyone at school called them the Three Musketeers. She was deep in thought about Paul. Maybe he'd ask her to homecoming next year. It could be fun to have a boyfriend, she thought as she kicked a stone with her toe.

Lindsey was so absorbed in thoughts of Paul she didn't notice the large van that pulled up next to her as she walked on the path along the lake. Suddenly, two big men jumped out, threw a large gunnysack over her head and body, and tossed her into the back of the van through the side door as if she were a bag of rocks. Her heart pounding, her lungs gasping for air, her mind racing, she struggled to grasp what was happening. She couldn't scream, but, reflexively, she kicked one of the men as hard as she could.

"Don't be stupid," one man said gruffly, "if you want to get out of this alive."

I

As Carley steered her car carefully down the lake road, her heart felt like it might leap out of her body. It had been two years since she had been back, and, in some ways, she had ached to return. In other ways, she wasn't at all sure she could face the pain she knew was waiting for her there. The people she loved most were gone—her father, who had died unexpectedly from a heart attack two years ago; her mother, who had died fourteen years earlier after a long battle with cancer; her brother, John, who had moved to California for a teaching position at USC; and Mac, her boyfriend who wasn't her boyfriend any longer. What would the lake be like without them?

Pulling into the gravel driveway of the cabin, Carley held her breath as the car rolled to a stop. Hesitantly, she got out of the car, worried that the magic she'd always felt here would be gone. As she scanned the property with its homey look and feel, she was surprised by how little had changed in two years. The garage, on the corner of the gravel driveway adjacent to the road, was surrounded by wild delphinium and a large raspberry patch with thousands of blossoms. A brick path led to the log cabin, an older home with a peaked roof and stone fireplace chimney. Under the shade of a gigantic oak tree stood the playhouse her father had built for her when she was little.

Her worry was needless. Immediately, she was overtaken by a sense of being totally centered, a sensation she didn't experience in any other part of her life, the feeling that no matter what terrible things were going on, she would be okay. She was home. Her anxiety and edginess started melting away.

In the light of dusk, she could see the lake, calm and settled. Tired from the long drive, she stretched her long legs and shook her slightly disheveled, short, sandy hair in the light lake breeze as if she were trying to cast off what was happening in her life. The sight of the lake, just as she'd remembered it, caused an unexpected ripple of exhilaration to bubble up inside her. Her Westie terrier, Abigail Rose, pushed past her and ran around the yard, thrilled to be released from the car. Carley walked to the edge of the water and stood there for some time, listening to a loon warbling, and watching the big, red fireball sun descend on the horizon. The air smelled like nowhere else—a distinct combination of fresh water, dead fish, cut grass, and wet wood. She inhaled it deeply. How could someplace stay so much the same when everything else was so chaotic? A fish jumped out of the water to snap up an insect. Of course, the calm surface was deceiving; there was a lot of chaos going on underwater too.

The beach was almost deserted because it was a Tuesday. Only a few lake residents stayed there during the week, even though most of them were from Fargo, just forty-five minutes away. If she lived that close, she would have moved here for the summer and commuted, but her home was in the Twin Cities several hours away—or at least it had been for the past twelve years, ever since she had graduated from college. This summer was different; this summer, she would live here. Now it was the only home she had.

Walking to the end of the dock, she took in the beautiful, edge-of-the-sunset moment with a horizon that had turned sky blue pink. A distant motorboat sped along the center of the lake, creating stripes that mirrored the sky. All in all, it was a beautiful evening.

The cabin had belonged to her family for generations; she'd inherited it from her father after his death. Her brother wasn't interested in it because it was too far for him to come. Unable to face her father's absence, she hadn't been back since his funeral. Joe, the handyman her father had hired, managed the property for her. He and his wife, Jean, were wonderful, making sure the dock and boat were in the water and everything was in working condition. For the past two summers, Joe had hoped Carley would change her mind and return, and he was elated when he got the call that she was coming.

The property wasn't expansive. Originally, most of the lakeshore was owned by a farmer who had unimaginatively sold off the land in small lots. Hers was one of the bigger ones, but it still wasn't large. That didn't matter to her. The proximity of neighbors was actually reassuring. Plus, it was all she had ever known.

Carley loved everything about the lake—swimming, fishing, water-skiing, long hikes, and early-evening cocktail cruises. She could taste the St-Germain that laced their gin and tonics as they puttered along near the shore, admiring and critiquing the other cottages, enjoying their well-loved, aging pontoon boat. Funny to call them cottages, she thought, when many of the older, small homes had been bulldozed and replaced by expansive log homes or mansions. She used to slalom behind the old pontoon, which probably looked odd from the beach, she mused. She had only happy memories here. It felt quiet, peaceful, good to be back.

A jet ski roared by, breaking her reverie. Feeling a small annoyance at the jarring sound of the motor, her eyes narrowed as she watched it glide noisily past her. *I would never own one of those*, she thought. Making her way back to the car to unpack her belongings, she called to Abigail Rose, who was sniffing a tree. Reaching into the back of the car, Carley took out the cage holding her cockatiel, Prattle, a beautiful yellow-and-gray bird who was glad to be out of the car but a little overwhelmed by the night chill and descending darkness.

It took a while to jiggle the key in the door lock, but reflexively, she hip-checked the door, and it swung open. She hadn't lost her touch.

The cabin had its usual slightly musty smell, not quite the smell of mold or mildew but not far removed. After all, the cabin was nearly eighty years old. Her great-grandfather had built it, and each generation had added something. Running water. Indoor plumbing. Her father had converted the large attic into a bedroom overlooking the lake, where she used to lie in bed at night listening to the waves lapping against the stone wall that held the yard back from the water. The first floor had an outdated kitchen with a large, round table where everyone used to gather to eat big meals, tell stories, and play games, a sturdy, rugged table made of oak, marred by years of use. It was hard to believe one piece of furniture could hold such memories. When she looked closer, she saw a note on the table and a big basket loaded with the largest, most luscious-looking blueberry muffins she had ever seen. From Joe and Jean, of course. They had taken the liberty of bringing in a few groceries, putting sheets on the bed, and cleaning things up to make sure she would feel at home. Their thoughtfulness swept over her, bringing tears she fought to choke back.

Setting the birdcage down, Carley got out a bowl and turned on the faucet. It worked, just as she knew it would, and soon the strong smell of well water wafted through the air. She filled the dish with water, setting it on the floor for Abigail, who lapped it up gratefully. Opening the creaky screen door, she went back out to her car for another load, while Abigail stood alertly by the back door, nervous she might be left behind. When Carley returned, she brought in the first of the boxes and set them on the table.

On her second trip to the car, she was startled to see a police car traveling fast down the dirt road behind her cabin. She hadn't seen a police car on that road before. It seemed oddly out of place. She hoped nothing was seriously wrong at the other end of the beach.

After eight trips, she had emptied everything out of the car, and soon the kitchen was overflowing with all she'd brought. She decided to put some of the boxes in her parents' room to get them out of the way.

Crossing the threshold of their bedroom was like retreating into her childhood. On the bed was the quilt her grandmother had made, on the walls were photos of her and John when they were little, and hanging over the bed was her mom and dad's wedding portrait. Nothing had changed since she had been here last. There wasn't a speck of dust anywhere, thanks to Jean, and the scent of lemon wood polish made it seem like her parents could walk through the door any minute. Readjusting the box, she decided to put it somewhere else.

Backing gently out of the bedroom, she scanned the living room with its rock fireplace, stone floor, and braided rug. The room was too beautiful to disrupt with boxes. John's bedroom, adjacent to her parents' room, was really the size of a large closet, a hole in the wall with bunk beds, his cowboy lamp, and glow-in-the-dark adhesive stars still adorning the ceiling. Better to store things here, out of the traffic flow.

Climbing the creaky wooden steps upstairs, she absorbed the view. The attic bedroom—her bedroom—had a high, peaked ceiling slanting off to the sides and expansive windows facing the lake that took up nearly the entire wall. Lying on her bed, she could see the lake. The opposite wall also had large, crank-out windows that overlooked the woods and the garage in back. Opening the windows, she felt the breeze begin to stir the musty air. She loved this room. Mac had been here once a few years back, and they had pushed the twin beds together. The thought of Mac made a lump rise in her throat as she choked down a small cough. Shaking the feeling off and pushing down the fear she felt about being alone, she went back down to get Abigail's bed and find a place for Prattle's cage, finally deciding the living room near the lake window would be a good place for the bird. When she called Abigail upstairs, the little dog came running.

Two hours later, with suitcases unpacked and her laptop, cell phone, and printer plugged in, she and Abigail fell onto the bed, tired, glad to be there, but drained from the emotion of coming back.

2

The girl lay stunned in a cold, dank room. One of the men pulled her up onto a chair, chaining her leg to the base. The men were talking excitedly, as if they hadn't expected to enjoy their heist as much as they had.

One man said to the others, "Hey, we might have a new gig here. Look at us. We did good. That was way more exciting than driving truck."

The second man grunted in agreement.

The third man didn't see it the same way as the other two, but he kept his mouth shut. He didn't mind what they'd been carrying for the past two years. Driving trucks was all he had ever done. Looking at the terrified girl, he wasn't proud. All this seemed so much riskier than what they had been transporting under the grain in their trucks. But the money was good, and he had said he'd do it. So now there was no going back.

3

The next morning, Carley awoke with a start. At first, she couldn't remember where she was or what she was doing there. It didn't take long for reality to rush in, with flashes of her job that was lost, her love that was over, her home that was gone. She wasn't sure she wanted to get out of bed. Abigail had other ideas.

Technically, she hadn't lost her job; when her company was bought out by a New York firm, they'd offered her a position if she would relocate, but when she'd declined, they had no choice but to let her go. Mac had been the main reason she had turned down the New York job. How ironic.

Shortly after that, she and Mac went their separate ways. It wasn't her idea. She'd been so absorbed with work during the buyout, she hadn't realized how little attention she was giving him. She loved her job and counted the people she worked with as family. There were fourteen-hour workdays and many going-away parties as most of the people she knew either relocated to New York or were terminated. She was so involved with the drama going on in her coworkers' lives, she wasn't aware of the drama unfolding in hers.

Mac, who played on a co-ed softball team, found the catcher much more available. Carley was caught completely off guard by his betrayal. It never would have occurred to her to turn to someone else if she had been in Mac's shoes. Why hadn't he told her how he felt? Why didn't he give her a chance to make it right? She had sold her condo to move into his; they had lived together for the past year and a half. Their breakup left her not only heartbroken, it left her without a place to live.

Fortunately, her layoff wasn't as bad as it might have been. When she was terminated, the company offered her a six-month consulting contract to prepare for a new product release. It would give her income during the transition and time to figure out what her next steps would be. She'd been too busy to even think about her career during the past several months. Here she was, thirty-four years old, without a job, without a love in her life, alone. The good news was that she could spend the summer at the lake, an opportunity she hadn't had since she was thirteen.

Later that morning, she gathered up her fishing gear, the carton of night crawlers Joe had left for her in the refrigerator, one of the large blueberry muffins, and Abigail's leash and made her way to the boat. She didn't have a fishing license, but she didn't think that would matter midweek. The DNR only patrolled the lake on weekends.

"Come on, girl," she called to Abigail, who immediately charged toward her.

They lazily drifted down Pelican Lake, through a channel toward Fish Lake, home to beautiful sunfish, northern pike, and a few bullheads. Memories of fishing there with her mother when she was young came flooding back. They would go out in a small rowboat with a five-horsepower motor at the crack of dawn, she at the helm. After a morning of fishing, they would bring back a stringer of large sunnies her dad would clean. As he showed off his work, he would always remark, "I should have been a brain surgeon." She smiled at the thought. He was such a brilliant man, he could have done anything he wanted. In the end, he chose teaching and research. It fit his personality. He was a favorite among students, not because he was the most dazzling professor but because he so genuinely cared about them, challenged them, and did anything he could to support them. He had been named the faculty member of the year four or five times that she could remember.

As Carley and Abigail approached the sandbar that separated one lake from the other, she was struck by how empty it was on a weekday. On the weekend, it would be loaded with teens from all over the lake meeting up and with parents who used to congregate on the sandbar as teens and brought their children there now. It was always crowded. Not today. She veered off to the left around a small island instead of driving over the sandbar. The adjoining Fish Lake was much less developed than Pelican. It had big bays surrounded by trees, dotted with beaver dams, and covered with lily pads. A few big homes were cropping up on the beach, but overall, Fish Lake remained less overrun. While she had heard rumors that a developer had purchased acres of property on Fish Lake to build a cluster of condominiums, she had hoped they were just that—rumors. Puttering near the shore, she was dismayed to see the sign, "Future site of Heron Bay Condominiums." So, it was true. She was surprised by the pit she felt in her stomach. It was the last unspoiled part of the lake, and she knew the construction would change the lake forever.

They continued until they reached the place where the lake narrowed to form a river. It was her favorite fishing spot of all— she had frequently caught northern and an occasional smallmouth bass there. Abigail settled down in the front of the boat, snapping distractedly at dragonflies.

Two hours later, they headed back to the cabin empty-handed. Carley had caught several perch, a few sunnies, and one very small northern and had thrown them all back. She was sad she hadn't caught any walleye. She really loved to eat fish, and walleye was her favorite. Nothing tasted better. Walleyes were safe that day.

As Carley and Abigail arrived home, they could hear Prattle chirping intensely in the cabin. Prattle seemed to think she was a dog, twittering frenetically whenever people came nearby—at least during the day. At night, the bird was as quiet as could be.

Carley left her pole and tackle box in the boat, deciding she might try fishing again later. However, she'd have to go to the local bait shop to get some minnows and a fishing license. She checked her cell phone to see if she'd had any calls. Just two—one from a director at her company giving her some changes in the product specifications, and the second from the lawn service she had tried to hire. It would be a few days before they could come out. Surveying the land around her cabin, she winced at the crop of dandelions that was beginning to flourish and hoped her neighbors wouldn't be too annoyed by the delay.

* * *

As Carley entered the bait shop, the familiar smell of wet wood struck her. *Bait shop* wasn't exactly the right description for the store. It had rows and rows of hardware, paint, motor equipment, fishing gear, a laundry and a small restaurant, along with a few groceries.

Just then, a man pushed past her, nearly knocking her over. It took Carley a second to recognize him. But when she did, she was startled. "Well, hi to you too, Hal!"

A thin, lanky, obviously distressed man glanced up at her and blanched. Clearly, he was caught off guard. "Oh, Carley. Wow. You're here. I didn't know you'd be back." He paused, staring at her intently. "Whatever they say, don't listen to them. They're wrong. It's not the way it looks."

With that, he put his head down and kept on going. Carley thought what an odd exchange it was. She'd known Hal Johnson since she was little; he was in her brother's grade. Her father had known him well; he was a junior faculty member in her father's department at the nearby university. Her father described him as "a man in search of ambition." She didn't think he had ever completed his PhD. She could see him teaching classes of freshmen— not too intense, not too demanding, nice enough. Although he was several years older than she, he had asked her out when they were in high school. She'd gone to a dance with him but later told him she'd rather they just stayed friends. They weren't really friends, but normally, he would have stopped to make a little small talk. After all, it had been over two years since she had seen him. Not today. And what he said made no sense at all. What could he possibly have meant?

Carley walked to the back of the bait shop to get the shiners. Since no one was around to help her, she went looking for a clerk. Several were huddled together, whispering nervously. *Good ol' small-town life*, she thought. No one was in a hurry to help. Finally, interrupting their conversation, she asked if she could trouble them for some assistance. Embarrassed, a young man about seventeen years old stepped forward to wait on her. Glancing at the pile of newspapers near the cash register, Carley spotted the headline: YOUNG WOMAN MISSING IN OTTER TAIL COUNTY. No wonder everyone was so distracted. The young woman must live nearby, which made it likely everyone here knew her. Carley shuddered, picked up her shiners and fishing license, paid what she owed, and left.

Returning to the cabin, she was surprised to see the garage door slightly ajar. She'd have to be more careful; feral cats, mice, and other critters would love to get inside. Opening the door, she peered into the darkness. The garage was overflowing with equipment, water skis, fishing poles, old lawn mowers, parts of a dock, blankets, tools, nuts, bolts, screws. Nothing seemed out of place, but, of course, nothing really had a place. Despite the clutter, the garage had such a familiar feeling to it—she could picture her father working here, puttering through a drawer, looking for a specific screw or nail. The sensation made her smile and a little sad at the same time. The tools that hung on the pegboard had been carefully arranged by size and type. The smell of oil was pervasive. Even though the lake home was over eighty years old, it hadn't shown its wear and tear until the last couple of years. Her father kept things in good working order.

She decided to put up the hammock and read for a while.

Abigail, now tethered to the same tree as the hammock, didn't appreciate being tied up, but it was a rule of the lake. With all the dogs around, Carley understood the need for some regulation. Abigail, on the other hand, didn't, and she went to the end of her rope, whimpering. Carley scooped Abigail into the hammock with her. After a while, they both fell asleep in the warm, sweet, muggy air with the rocking motion of the hammock.

* * *

Carley awoke with a chill. By her hunger pangs, she could tell it must be getting late. Abigail looked up at her expectantly. "Oh, sure, all you have to do is look at me with those great big eyes," she teased. "I have to do all the work. Let's go figure out what's for dinner." With that, she went inside, Abigail trotting closely behind, until they reached the door. Carley removed the tether, and Abigail jumped in the door ahead of her. "Glad I didn't slow you down," she said to the eager dog.

Inside the cabin, Prattle was pacing back and forth in her cage.

"Oh, not you too," Carley mused.

Everyone was hungry. She got out ground beef and made two and a half patties. Even the bird liked hamburger. She went out into the garage, found the grill, and rolled it out near the house. Now all she needed was the propane tank, hopefully with some propane. Knowing her dad, she was sure she would find one filled. However, the propane tank was nowhere to be found, not that it was easy to find anything in the garage. While her dad had always kept everything in good shape, he was a pack rat. Digging under a pile of boxes and blankets, she came up empty-handed.

From the corner of her eye, she caught a glimmer of movement and, spinning around, saw a large, hulking figure standing silently in the doorway of the garage. She gasped. She was cornered—there was no other way out.

4

Instinctively, she grabbed a nearby shovel for protection.

"Sorry—I didn't mean to startle you," the big, lumbering man said with a drawl. It was her neighbor a few cabins down, whom she'd known since they were both in grade school.

As relief flooded over, her knees went weak. Recent events had her nerves on alert. "I didn't see it was you, Ben," she admitted. "What are you doing here?"

"Well, I thought I'd come down and say hello. It's been quite a while since you've been here. Bet you've got a lot of work to do."

"Yeah, it's a little overwhelming," she agreed. Ben always offered to help, but once he was around, it seemed like forever until he left. "I'm missing a propane tank. Any chance you have a spare you could loan me until tomorrow?"

"Sure," he said. And off he went to get one.

After a few minutes, Ben returned, dragging a wagon with a propane tank. He'd packed on a lot of weight since she had last seen him, and he was breathing hard because of the exertion. "Here, this should do the trick," he said.

Gratefully, she accepted the tank and attached it to her grill. As she pushed the automatic igniter, she smiled. It worked! She closed the cover of the grill, allowing it time to heat up before she put the burgers on. Ben sat down and picked up a hammer, examining it closely.

"Thanks, Ben," she said. "So, what's new around here?"

Glad for the interest she was showing, Ben thought hard about what she might consider news. "Well, we're getting a new road out here. We've really needed one for a long time." Carley nodded. "The potholes have been getting pretty deep." He paused, trying to think of other things of interest. "And, of course, there's the missing girl."

"The missing girl? Who is she?" Carley asked. "Anyone you know?"

"Sure, I know her. Everyone around here does. Her name is Lindsey. She used to work at the bait shop."

Oh, Carley thought. *No wonder everyone there seemed a bit off this morning. They knew the girl. They were afraid for her.* She shuddered. Hardly anything like that ever happened around here. The last missing person had been related to the lawyer who lived a few cabins away. It was his wife. There was considerable speculation about what had happened to her, though the lawyer insisted she had run off to New York to get away from small-town life. No body was ever found, so she concluded he was probably right. That was over twenty years ago.

As smoke rose from the grill, Carley said, "Well, I'd better go get a platter to put these burgers on. Thanks, Ben, for your help. I'll drop the tank off tomorrow, if that's okay with you."

Ben nodded, looking disappointed that she didn't want to talk more. Smiling at her, he said, "Of course. Don't be a stranger now. I didn't mean to scare you before. It's good to have someone up here. Let me know if I can help." Off he lumbered.

Carley turned to Abigail Rose and said, "Come on, girl; it's time for dinner." In they went. While Ben had been a big help, she was glad to see him go.

The next day, Carley awoke with an uneasy feeling. She had expected to feel more settled here, but the uneasiness of her life had followed her. She had slept fitfully, dreaming about people from work, of Mac with his new girlfriend, about the young girl who was missing. In her dream, she found the girl, but she was muffled. She couldn't yell, she couldn't cry, she couldn't call out for help. Carley was glad to awaken, with Abigail sitting on the end of her bed, waiting for her to get up and feed her. Ah, reality! It was a surprisingly welcome relief.

After breakfast, Carley stretched and said, "Well, girl, I hate to leave you, but I have to go back to the bait shop to get a new battery for the boat." From the way the motor had sputtered to start the day before, she knew the battery had spent too much time in the frozen garage over the past two winters. The motor probably needed new spark plugs too, but those would have to wait until she could figure out how to change them.

Opening the door, she was surprised to see the newspaper on the step. She had ordered newspaper service online just the day before, and there it was. Impressive. Not all services up here worked quite that efficiently.

The headline was startling: STEPFATHER INTERROGATED ABOUT MISSING GIRL. The story was accompanied by a picture of Hal Johnson. She was dumbfounded. No wonder Hal had looked so pale. She read further and realized it was his stepdaughter, Lindsey, who was missing. She hadn't connected those dots before, and her stomach roiled at the thought. She'd known Lindsey as a young girl. Her father had invited Hal, his new wife, Sarah, and Hal's stepdaughter, Lindsey, to the lake for a barbecue. Carley had taught her how to water-ski. Lindsey must have been about ten years old back then. She knew Lindsey didn't care for Hal, but that was understandable. He was an interloper who took her mother's attention away from her. Knowing it was this little Lindsey who was missing was disturbing.

Carley just couldn't believe Hal could hurt a flea. She remembered him being passive, very laid-back. He had never acted inappropriately that she could remember. It made her shudder. Would it be like him to hurt his stepdaughter? She didn't think so, but she didn't know what to believe. *Why did he even venture out in public?*

He probably doesn't think of the bait shop as "the public." His words came flooding back to her. "It's not the way it looks," he had said. She hoped that was true. But why would he bother saying that? Really, did he care what she thought?

Her cell phone jolted her back to her other world. It was the VP of marketing, who had an idea he wanted to run by her and wanted an update on what she was doing. After a ten-minute conversation, the VP was satisfied she was headed in the right direction with the marketing initiative and had left her with his pearls of wisdom. She had to make him feel good about his ideas, even though they were usually somewhat lame. Oh, the joys of corporate life. She wouldn't miss the politics she had to maneuver through. This VP was a good guy. Still, he was fairly clueless, she mused.

When her phone rang again, it was Trish, her closest friend from the Twin Cities.

"How are you doing up there in the hinterlands? Are you coming back soon? I miss you!" Trish moaned.

Carley said dryly, "I've only been up here a day. Really, I'll have to give it a little longer than that."

Trish laughed. "How does it feel to be back? Are you doing okay?"

Carley responded, "It's better than I'd expected. The lake is beautiful, and the weather has been unusually warm for June. I miss everyone, including you, so let me know when you can come up here. The sooner the better."

"Yeah, I imagine it's pretty dull," Trish said.

"*Dull* isn't exactly right. A girl I knew from a small town up here was abducted. They don't have a clue what's happened to her. Pretty scary stuff."

"Really? You know her?"

"Not well, but her father worked with my father."

"Wow. Small world. Are you worried being there alone?"

"Not really. I mean, it's a little quiet around here during the week when no one's around. But, no, I'll be fine. I can defend myself. Just get yourself up here."

Trish promised she would.

"Yes, I'm really going out the door," Carley turned to Abigail Rose.

* * *

At the bait shop, things were a little more settled than they had been the day before. There were more customers in the store, not surprising since it was almost the weekend. The newspapers were all sold out—due to the local news, Carley assumed. She was glad she had thought to start up the delivery. She talked with a salesclerk about what size battery she needed for the boat and about how to change the spark plugs in her motor. She picked up a half gallon of milk, a bag of M&M's, and some dog treats.

As she stood in line at the checkout, a woman walked into the store and started to shriek when she saw Carley. *Yikes*, Carley thought. *It isn't easy to blend into the woodwork around here.*

"*Carley! Carley!* You're back!" she squealed. Mary hadn't lost her cheerleading exuberance.

"Hi, Mary! Look at you!" Mary looked as disgustingly good as she had when they were in high school together.

"It's been forever since I've seen you around here. What are you up to these days?"

"Well, I had a once-in-a-lifetime opportunity to move up here for the summer to work on a consulting project, and I just had to take it." She thought that was a better answer than *I'm jobless, loveless, and a little lost right now.* "How about you?"

"Oh, Steve and I just bought a new lake home on Lake Lida. We have three children—two boys and a girl. So, life is busy. Can you believe all that's happening around here? Ha! Who would have thought he'd be involved with anything like this? In school, he never got in any trouble that I can remember. I mean, he was usually quiet and not exactly popular. He was socially awkward, but he just didn't seem like someone who would hurt a fly. I just can't believe all he's being accused of. Can you? Didn't you two go out a couple of times?"

"Just once." She didn't want to tell Mary what Hal had said when she saw him. Somehow, she just didn't want to fuel the speculation that was going on.

"Well, obviously you were smart! Gotta run. You'll have to stop by and see us sometime."

Carley agreed she would, knowing full well that was highly unlikely.

5

She felt the blade of a knife pressed against her throat. She gasped. Was he going to kill her? What was he going to do? Her heart pounding, her small voice pleaded, "Please, don't."

The man said, "What, does this scare you? It should." He laughed out loud and shoved the blindfolded girl back on the floor. "Just you wait," he said as he lumbered across the room and slammed the metal door behind him.

The girl lay motionless on the concrete floor whimpering, hardly daring to breathe, trembling all over. She had no idea where she was or what she was doing there. Hours earlier, she had been walking with her friends. Why had they taken her? What could they possibly want?

He was gone, at least for now. So were the other two. No one had done anything to her—yet. That was good. She tried to commit their hulking figures to her memory, but they were so similar she couldn't tell them apart—big, burly men who swore a lot and smelled like chewing tobacco. Disgusting, dirty, crude, brash, strong. All she really knew was that they scared her. Her mind was swirling. Could she get the blindfold off? The rope that tied her wrists together? Could she get away if she got loose? Where was she? Panic rose in her throat like bile. The most important thing she needed to do was concentrate on surviving. Surely someone would find her.

6

Carley got up early the next morning. She loved not having to go to an office, but she'd only been at the lake for two days, and already she was feeling disconnected from her world.

Mac dominated her thoughts. How she missed him, the fun they'd had together--playing almost any kind of sport, talking over a glass of wine at night, cooking together. Mac had been there for her when her father had died. She wondered how he was doing with his new friend.

It had been a long time since she'd felt that much pain. She couldn't believe he'd cheated on her. Not only had they talked about marriage, she considered him her soul mate. She never would have betrayed him like that, and she didn't think he could go behind her back as he had. Better to find out now what his true staying power was. While intellectually that made sense, the ache in her heart made her wonder how she would ever stop thinking about him. Would she take him back if he changed his mind? She couldn't imagine that right now either.

It would be a long time before she would consider having another relationship. On the other hand, she wasn't sure Abigail Rose and Prattle could really provide satisfying relationships, much as she loved them both.

When she sat down to work on the new product release, her ideas came quickly. She'd done this so many times before. She had a good intuitive sense plus a strong background in marketing that helped her present ideas well. The last product launch had been a huge success, luckily, or she would be completely out of work right now. She had to call one of the company engineers to get some information clarified. "Hi, Mike," Carley said.

"Well, hey there, pretty lady. How are things going up at the lake?" he drawled.

"Well enough," she answered. Normally, she would have reeled at being called "pretty lady," but she knew Mike well—he was a gem of a person. They had worked closely together for over six years, and she always trusted his work—and him. He took time to explain complex technical issues to her. She appreciated that. And he trusted her keen marketing sense. Quickly they got down to business, she got the information she needed, and they signed off.

She worked for a few more hours, losing herself in what she was doing. Suddenly, she realized it was 1:00 in the afternoon and she hadn't had lunch yet. Abigail Rose was getting restless. Carley pulled out the leash, and Abigail came running. It was a two-mile stretch to the café at the store. She really shouldn't take much time away from her work right now, but she didn't feel like fixing lunch. So off they hiked.

* * *

When they arrived at the café, the air was electric. Carley could tell something big had happened. Stopping one of the store clerks, she asked, "What's going on? I've never seen this place buzz like this."

"You know the girl who's been missing? Her stepdad was arrested yesterday in the parking lot. He shops here all the time. Nobody can believe it. Everybody has some theory about what he's done and why he did it."

"What's he done? Couldn't Lindsey just be missing? Did the police find something? What if she's just off on her own, out for a good time?" She didn't want to think of Hal doing anything to harm anyone.

The clerk shook his head. "I don't know. I haven't heard anything more, but they must have found something. I've never seen anyone handcuffed in real life."

Deciding it was too disturbing to stay at the café, she and Abigail traipsed back home, a little worn out. Excited by their return, Prattle chirped and chirped to signal their arrival. It was a good contrast to the distress at the café. The events were intruding on her idyllic view of life at the lake.

* * *

By evening, Carley had to admit she had accomplished almost nothing all day. Her head was swirling with ideas for the new product launch, but none of them were quite right. Her head was swirling about Hal and his stepdaughter. Nothing about that fit what she knew. Her head was swirling about her own life, and nothing about that made sense either. Except that she was at the lake and glad to be there, she felt unusually adrift.

That night, the lake was like glass, and the sky was lit with stars. It was so calm she decided to take the kayak out on the water. Dark, quiet, and muggy, it was a perfect night for a ride. She dragged the kayak down to the lake from the garage, arming herself with bug spray and two flashlights—one she wore around her head like a miner would, the other a rechargeable spotlight big enough to signal a boat coming from any direction. To keep the mosquitoes at bay, she kept the lights off. There were no boats in sight and not likely to be many out this late at night since it was about 10:00 p.m. on a weekday. This time, she left Abigail Rose behind, much to the dog's dismay, but Carley didn't want to bring her and risk tipping over.

The kayak glided quietly over the calm, moonlit water. It was fun to be out in the night and so invisible. She glanced at the cabins as she slid by them. Most of them were dark. The very few that were occupied had people watching TV. She felt a bit like a voyeur as she moved effortlessly down the beach, venturing out farther into the lake, which was as calm as glass.

After paddling quite a distance, she heard voices—men's voices—in the darkness. She was going to turn on one of her lights, but she couldn't tell whether the voices were coming from the beach or a boat. Lifting her paddle from the water, she rested it on the front of the kayak while she got her bearings. Ahead in the water, she could just make out the outline of a pontoon. She couldn't tell who the men were or even what they looked like. The haze of the night made it impossible to see much of anything.

Talking in deep, low voices, the men were calling to each other in raspy whispers. "Over here," one voice said. "You've got to push from your side."

She could make out three shapes on a darkened pontoon boat about fifty yards out from where she was. They were throwing—or rather pushing—something into the lake. Whatever it was, two of them were awkwardly maneuvering a large, long bag over the side of the boat. Why were they out there with no lights? What could they possibly be doing? Could that be a body bag? She turned around, paddled back to the shore by her cabin as quickly as she could, and tugged the kayak carefully up the embankment.

Her heart was pounding in her ears. Carley didn't seem to have caught anyone's attention on the boat, and for that she was very grateful. What were they up to? What were they throwing off the boat? Could she recognize any of the men? None of them saw her, she was quite certain. Apprehensively, she made her way back to the cabin.

What she didn't see was the man three cabins down watching her through his binoculars.

7

The next morning, Carley was stewing about what she had seen the night before, trying to make sense of it. The most benign thing she could think of was that someone was throwing concrete from a construction project or a big motor wrapped in plastic into the lake. Her worst fear was that it was a body wrapped in a tarp. What if it was Lindsey? Should she alert someone about what she'd seen? Probably she had been watching too much TV. While they likely shouldn't have been dumping what they were dumping, that didn't necessarily make them criminals. People threw things into the lake all the time. Her own father had taken chunks of concrete he had removed from the old floor of the garage and deposited those in the middle of the lake, certain it wouldn't hurt anyone. She didn't think it would pose any problems either; other people had dumped motors or worse. The most unusual thing she had heard that had been found in the water was a mechanical bull, the kind that was in a country music bar. No one could figure out how it got there—or why.

Still, the scene gnawed at her. If it wasn't something illicit, why were they doing it in the dark of night? She decided to clear her mind by going for a run.

As she put on her running shoes, Abigail Rose excitedly retrieved her leash, thinking they were both going. They weren't. Carley knew it would be too far for little Abigail Rose's legs to carry her, and she was too heavy for Carley to carry if she couldn't make it. Carley went out the door despite Abigail's protests and ran down the road away from the beach, eventually moving effortlessly past a farmhouse, a hunting stand, and a slough filled with cattails. It was a beautiful day, perfect for a three-mile run. She fell into an easy cadence, breathing in the fresh, fragrant air.

As she came over a hill, the sprawl of a trucking business on the property of one of the farmers loomed up like a metal jungle. Hank Larson still farmed the land, but now he had five tractor trailers and a junkyard full of parts that were an eyesore on the otherwise green and rolling hills. Across the road from this mess was his beautiful lake home. She vaguely wondered how he could afford it, given that his farm wasn't that large. Hank, a heavy drinker, was always angry and irritable with people on the beach. She could resonate with how life's circumstances could make one edgy. Still, the house was great, probably the work of his ex-wife.

There was a small gaggle of wild turkeys and a few cows ahead. As the scenery again became bucolic, she put everything out of her mind and concentrated on the beauty around her. It was picturesque—a world apart from all the chaos she knew in the Cities. She loved running and the peaceful state of mind it created.

Her reverie was interrupted by a police car driving speedily by her. It was a disarming sight, the second time she'd seen a police car on this road. The car pulled quickly into Hank Larson's driveway. She wondered what Hank's son was up to now.

* * *

When she finished her run, she came into the cabin to hear Prattle chirping at the top of her lungs and Abigail Rose barking excitedly at her return. "Girls, girls." She marveled at the cacophony that greeted her. Once she was inside, the pets settled back down. "Ha." She chuckled. "No human has ever greeted me with that much enthusiasm!"

The run had cleared her mind. Deciding that she should let the police figure out whether what she saw was worth exploring or not, she called the Pelican Rapids police department and asked to speak to the sheriff, Tom Bradshaw.

"I don't know if it means anything," Carley said. "I just thought you should know."

"I doubt that it's anything," the sheriff said after she described what she'd observed. "People dump things into the lake they shouldn't all the time. We have a lot on our plates right now with the missing girl; we don't have time to worry about what garbage people are throwing in the lake. But thanks for calling. Let me know if you see anything else suspicious."

Carley, caught off guard by how quickly he had dismissed her concerns, felt sheepish for having called. Most likely she was over-reacting. It was difficult not to, given all that was happening in the area. The sheriff was condescending, which she didn't understand or especially appreciate. While she didn't know him well, she had seen him around town at the coffee shop. He was an average-height man with a bulging stomach and a big, bold laugh, a man who didn't move too fast, a man with a swag when he walked. Would he follow up on her call? What if he didn't? Although she had done her part, it didn't feel like enough.

* * *

She had a difficult time regaining the focus on her work. She tried unsuccessfully to sketch out a timeline for the product release. After several attempts, she set her work aside. Cleaning a closet was about all the concentration she could muster. Plus, it helped her work out some of her frustration about the sheriff's response. Her head hurt from trying not to think about what the men had pushed off their boat. Finally, she gave up feeling guilty about her lack of productivity. The hammock was calling her.

Carley rocked back and forth absent-mindedly while Abigail Rose sniffed the ground around her and chased a beetle. It was a glorious day. With the wind from the south, the lake in front of her was calm, the air hot and dry. Abigail finally settled down and lay down next to her.

Suddenly, Abigail jumped to her feet, barking excitedly. Around the corner of the cabin came a man in a white shirt and dress pants. Immediately, he put up his hand and said, "Sorry. I didn't mean to scare you! My name is Jeff Barnes, and I'm a Realtor in the area. I heard you might need one, so thought I would stop by and introduce myself."

"What makes you think I need a Realtor?" she asked, puzzled.

"One of your neighbors down the beach told me you had recently returned. He figured this place might be too much for you to handle. I understand you don't live near here."

"Well, I do now," she responded. *Ha, funny inference*, she thought. She didn't know anyone down the beach was even aware she was here. "I just moved here for the summer. I really don't have any intention of selling. This cabin has been in my family since it was built. And, no, it isn't too much for me to handle."

"I didn't mean to insult you. Owning a cabin is much more challenging than most people realize. It seems like something is always going wrong. I sell a lot of lakeshore property, and I'm always trying to get a jump on my competition, so just thought I'd ask. It's a nice place—at least from the outside. Very rustic."

She laughed. "Rustic—isn't that code for 'needs a lot of work'?"

He smiled. "No, I really like it. It has warmth but isn't overdone. So many places now are overbuilt—huge, lavish homes that no one has the time to live in. Oops, I almost forgot. Here's my card, in case you change your mind. Or maybe sometime you'd like someone to do something with. I can help there too." He smiled.

She studied his card. *Did this man almost ask me out?* She chuckled. Well, not exactly, but he certainly opened the door. He was tall, good-looking enough, blond. Not quite her type. She liked men who were a little less polished, a little more rugged. But perhaps they could do something fun sometime. God knew she could use the company. "I'll remember that," she acknowledged, smiling.

8

It was Friday, and Carley was glad the beach was filling up again. She could hear cars driving in and the buzz of boats coming out on the water. Kids were screaming a few doors down. The lake was coming to life. It was good timing; she wasn't sure how much longer she could hold out without someone to talk to. While she loved the lake and the calm she felt there, she had a hollow feeling in her stomach she couldn't quite explain. Maybe it was that stupid boat in the middle of the night. Maybe it was just loneliness.

She gave her next-door neighbors an hour to get settled after they arrived before she walked over with a bottle of red wine.

When Jana opened the front door, she shouted, "Woo-hoo! Dan, look who the cat dragged in! Hi, Carley!" They hugged.

Dan came over and gave her a big hug too. She was glad to see them. She and Jana had grown up on the lake together. Dan was going to cook steaks and asked Carley if she could join them. She was dying for a little familiar conversation.

* * *

They finished off the bottle of red wine, then another, and, finally, the steaks. Their conversation covered the usual topics of how things were going with their jobs (or lack thereof), with their families, with the beach. Jana's mother was the beach captain, so

Jana and Dan knew the scoop on all the new neighbors. They talked briefly about Hal. Jana knew of Hal, but with an age difference of six years, she really didn't know him well. Her news was from Fargo, where Hal worked. He'd been put on administrative leave by the university until everything was sorted out. Everyone assumed he was guilty. Carley really felt for him—if there were a mob, he would be hanged by now.

* * *

The sunset was a glorious reddish pink when Carley went back to her cabin. It felt good to have a conversation with people she cared about. She hadn't seen them since her dad's funeral, so they'd had a lot to catch up on. Jana told her that the annual beach association meeting was scheduled for the next morning.

The beach association meeting was an annual event that consisted of neighbors who were happy to see one another but really didn't care if they saw one another again for the rest of the summer. There were benefits in banding together—specifically, mosquito spraying and road repair. Everyone was glad to reconnect but didn't want to become too close. After all, the purpose of having a lake home was having a getaway with no obligations.

This year, the meeting had the usual agenda items and three new ones: zebra mussels, the condo development on Fish Lake, and the disappearance of Hal's stepdaughter. The beach association was concerned about safety. Sheriff Bradshaw gave a quick update on the search for Lindsey and what to do if anyone saw anything suspicious. Carley laughed to herself that it would have to be something quite dramatic before she'd call the sheriff again. If pushing something off a boat in the dark with no lights on wasn't suspicious, what would be? She shook her head in disbelief. One of the neighbors suggested having a neighborhood watch system, just as everyone had at home in Fargo. Neighborhood watches really didn't stop anything, she thought. But everyone did agree that anything out of the ordinary should be reported to both the sheriff and to the beach captain, Jana's mom.

The condo project was moving forward. Prints of the proposed condo buildings were taped to the side of the garage of the president's lake home, showing five buildings that would have forty condos each, plus a small restaurant and boat gas station. Murmuring from the crowd indicated its general disapproval. One man asked if there was anything that could be done to stop construction. The consensus was it was too late for that. The lake association, comprised of over fifteen beach associations on the lake, had hired an attorney and tried to fight it when it came up for a vote before the county zoning and planning commission about nine months earlier. The county didn't oppose it because of the tax revenue the condos would generate. The project easily passed, despite the outpouring of public objection to how adding the expected five hundred–plus residents and their visitors would stress the lake and destroy the only pristine area left. The zebra mussel problem seemed more controllable.

A sudden cloudburst broke up the meeting; everyone grabbed their lawn chairs and scattered back to their respective lake homes. The storm continued throughout the day, so even though it was a weekend, Carley concentrated on her work. All lake activity came to a grinding halt because of the lightning. Abigail sulked around the cabin. The thunderous backdrop made Prattle nervous, and she paced anxiously back and forth across her perch.

The gloomy day melted into an even gloomier night. Carley felt an emptiness she hadn't faced for a long time. She curled up in a chair to read a book but couldn't concentrate. She found herself staring off, thinking about Mac, thinking about her dad, wishing life were different. Her melancholy gave way to big, heavy sobs. It wasn't like her to feel so desolate. Normally, she was feisty, determined, ready for any anything. She already didn't recognize her life, and now she didn't recognize herself.

9

By Sunday evening, everyone—well, almost everyone—had left the beach. Where was their sense of adventure? she wondered. Abigail Rose and Prattle would have to do in the meantime.

She was puzzled by how she might create a social life here. Church? Maybe. A bar? Really not her thing. Bridge? She could hardly remember how to play. She could look online. Ha. She had almost no interest in dating right now. She wished she had female friends in the vicinity, but she didn't. Her once-active social life had come to a screeching halt. Even in the city where she lived, many of her friends had moved away or were married with children, which was as good as moving away. Trish and Mac were the extent of her close friends, outside of people from work. She winced at how she had let Mac dominate her life. There were other women she had as friends—her book club, a group at church. But they were on the periphery, not the mainstream, of her life. "Minnesota nice" was real. People were polite but very difficult to get to know.

She decided she would explore sailing lessons and golf. Maybe that would distract her from the things that were bothering her.

She wondered how the lake survived the stress of the boat traffic weekend after weekend. The wind was from the south, so it was very calm on her side of the lake, but it was overcast and quite wavy about a hundred yards from shore. Deciding to go for a boat ride, she invited Abigail Rose to come along. The great thing about the dog is that Carley didn't have to ask twice. Abigail jumped on board, and off they went.

The lake was settling back to its pre-weekend calm. Boats were tightly wound up on their lifts, few grills were smoking, and no dogs were barking. The Adirondack chairs on patios were empty. Almost everyone had headed back to town. She proceeded down the lake to the one place that gassed up boats. It closed in just a few minutes, and she wanted to get there in time.

She pushed the button near the gas pump, and soon two young women came, chatting as they slowly made their way down the dock. She felt a sense of impatience rising inside her but forced it back down. They were friendly but nervous. Suddenly, it occurred to her that they were the same age as the missing girl.

"Hey," one of the girls said to her.

"Hey there," Carley responded. "How are you on this beautiful evening?"

The girls shrugged and said, "We're okay."

"Just okay?" Carley watched them intently as they started pumping the gas.

"I guess. You know the girl from Vergas who's missing? She's a friend of ours."

"Lindsey? How do you know her? Do you go to the same school?"

"No, but a group of us were supposed to go to church camp together this week with her. It's scary."

Carley agreed. The whole thing was very distressing. "Did she ever talk about her stepfather?" Carley asked. She felt she shouldn't ask that question, but she couldn't resist.

"They don't get along very well. Lindsey doesn't like him. She says he took her mother away from her."

"I don't know. He seemed nice enough to me," the other girl replied.

Carley continued, "Do you think she might have just gone off on her own?"

"No way," the girls said in unison.

One added, "She's pretty straight. She doesn't drink or smoke or do drugs. She doesn't even have a boyfriend. She's just a really, really good person."

Just as they were finishing the transaction, another pontoon boat pulled up for gas. As Carley began to push away from the dock, the sound of the motor caught her attention. Quickly, she turned and looked behind her. Two men were maneuvering the pontoon closer to the pump. Was that how the pontoon she'd heard a couple of nights ago sounded?

Her mind raced to remember anything about the pontoon. It was so dark and hazy that night, and there were so few lights on around the lake she hadn't been able to see much. She had a vague memory of the shape of the boat, but that was about all. This pontoon had the same outline, but so did most of the pontoons on Pelican. Hers didn't, only because it was about ten years older than this model.

Watching her stare intently at their boat, the driver gave her a half wave. She thought she recognized the man as a neighbor down the beach. Was it the attorney? She'd only met him once and couldn't be sure. His reputation was that he was a shark in court. However, she couldn't imagine him throwing a body out of his pontoon decked with fishing equipment.

Clearly, she needed a diversion. Tomorrow she would check out sailing lessons at the yacht club across the lake. *Yacht club* was a misnomer—it was a trailer on a small lot with a raft of sailboats moored nearby. She used to sail on a little Sailfish when she was young. Perhaps a new challenge would absorb some of her restlessness. Maybe she would give Jeff, the Realtor, a call to invite him to join her. She'd see.

Her mind kept going back to Mac. There was no question that they had had a connection, they'd had chemistry, they'd fit with each other. But it went way beyond that. They had planned their future together. He was her "every day"—the one who knew the little things of her life, who knew her innermost thoughts and feelings. She told him everything; she thought he did the same with her. He was a great listener, and his opinion mattered to her. She was so sure of his love for her that she had taken it for granted.

They'd just seemed so right for each other. They had planned their lives together—two great careers, two or three children, a house on a lake. Both had good jobs, loved music and sports, were avid readers. They hardly ever fought. Perhaps that was the problem. If Mac had just told her how he felt, maybe things would have worked out differently. She felt stupid for not knowing, embarrassed, humiliated. But mostly, she was very, very lonely, not sure where life would take her. Starting over was challenging. While she knew she could do it, it just seemed so daunting. It was difficult to see the life ahead of her. And she really, really missed him. Choking back tears, she knew she had to find a way to stop thinking about him. It was time to get on with her life.

10

The next morning, with new resolve, Carley decided she should at least see what kind of jobs were out there. She was feeling pressure to get going on her job search. While she had a small nest egg from her father and some savings of her own, she didn't want that to be eaten up by everyday expenses. First, she had to decide where she wanted to work. On a whim, she decided to look at jobs in Fargo. While her best contacts were in the Twin Cities, it seemed less stressful to start locally. Researching companies in Fargo, she came up with four or five she thought might have positions for someone with her skills. They were industrial manufacturers, producing everything from snowmobiles to construction materials and agricultural products.

After a couple of hours, overwhelmed by the search, she went online to explore options for sailing and golf. The intermediate sailing class wasn't starting for three weeks. She decided to sign up anyway, hoping her experience with a Sailfish qualified her for that level, even if it had been fifteen years earlier. At least she understood the fundamental principles of sailing.

Golf was another story. Her athleticism seemed to fail her in this sport; a good swing had always eluded her. She preferred volleyball, the sport she'd played in college, to this game where the ball stood still. But since sailing was a few weeks off and there were no volleyball teams in sight, she decided she might as well try golf. There was a best-ball scrambler advertised for Saturday at the public course about twenty minutes away, and she could take a refresher before the scrambler started. She signed up, feeling a bit sorry for the team that got her, rationalizing that at least it was a chance to be outside with people. She knew she needed that.

The next morning, Carley went over to the golf course to hit balls. It had been over three years since she'd had her clubs out of the garage. The last time she'd golfed had been with her father. He was a strong golfer, yet patient with her. He gave her tips, but she really needed to take lessons. She never had; she thought she could pick up the sport more easily than she had. She'd better remember what little she knew so she wouldn't completely embarrass herself at the tournament.

Walking into the clubhouse of the golf course, she approached the counter. "A large bucket, please," she said. Approaching the bulletin board, she perused the ad for golf lessons. There was an adult group starting up at 10:00 a.m. After glancing at her watch, she decided she'd stick around to see if it was a good opportunity. "Is it full?" she asked.

"Naw," the young man behind the counter responded. "You can join up now if you want."

* * *

As she teed up the ball, she breathed in the smell of the freshly mowed grass. The course was beautifully manicured, the day gorgeous. There was a fair amount of wind—there had been white-caps on her side of the lake that morning. But that didn't matter for what she was doing. She hit the ball and was pleased when she connected. It went over 150 yards. The next ball barely dribbled ahead. Unfortunately, she never knew if the ball was going to go flying or if she would send it off into the woods, never to be seen or heard from again. She looked around to see who else was there. There was a man in his sixties, surely a retired executive, who had a beautiful, well-honed swing. Next to him was a teenager who probably played on a high school golf team. He was quite good. On the third tee was another man she recognized from the beach association meeting. She hadn't met him yet; he'd seemed aloof during the buzz about all that was happening. He was a good-looking guy a few years older than she, dark hair, glasses, serious looking. Tilting her head down, she kept on swinging. The man looked up absent-mindedly, did a slight double take when he spotted her, then went back to the shot he was trying to perfect. *A golf course is a good place to feel like you're with people, even when you aren't, and the scenery makes it worthwhile*, she thought.

At 10:00 a.m., she went out and joined the pro who would be teaching the class. In his early twenties and quite good looking, he knew it was important for him to get the enrollees to like him. That would create opportunities for one-on-one sessions, where he made the most money. In addition to Carley, there was a woman in her sixties who was golfing for the first time, a man in his forties who wanted to learn how to golf for business, and a young woman of sixteen who had about as much skill as Carley did. The pro explained it didn't matter where they were skill-wise. He was starting with the fundamentals, since that's where most people go wrong. He had them each hit a few balls so he could assess what help they needed. Carley whiffed a couple, then connected on one. "Nice shot," he remarked. She felt like there was hope that she wouldn't make a complete fool of herself.

By the end of the morning, the woman in her sixties had signed up for one-on-one sessions with the pro. Carley felt like she'd made progress on both her swing and her stance. She should have waited to hit balls until after the lesson. Oh well; she'd try again tomorrow.

When she returned home, she was startled to see the door to the garage door ajar. Quite certain she had shut it before she left, she was a little apprehensive about going into the dark expanse. It added to the growing sense of uneasiness she had had for the last few days. It was time to buy a lock for the door. Why would anyone want to break into her garage? Outside of a collection of worn hand tools, her father's filing cabinet, and a lot of junk, there wasn't much of value there. As she peered inside, she couldn't see anything missing.

She called the police from her cell phone. While she felt sheepish reporting a non-crime, she felt very uneasy about someone breaking in. The police said they would come over and check it out. She could hear Prattle chirping away in the cabin.

It took a while for the police to get there. Of course, she realized it was a small force, and she was sure they were heavily tied up with the girl's disappearance, as well they should be. Feeling a little guilty for even calling them, she was relieved it was a junior officer, not the sheriff she'd talked to earlier, who showed up and went through the garage with her. Again, nothing seemed out of place. It was eerie just the same. She asked if they had any clues to Lindsey's disappearance.

"No, nothing concrete," said the officer. He then proceeded to tell her how they hadn't had a case like this in the county in years. The last one involved moonshine, nothing like a missing person. Oh, and the disappearance of the lawyer's wife. The nice young cop suggested she get a deadbolt installed on the garage door. Carley agreed that was a good idea.

* * *

It wasn't until later that day that she realized what someone might have been looking for. She went to start up the grill and found the propane tank still there. Probably it was just Ben looking for the one he'd loaned her, though she wondered why he wouldn't look on the grill instead of going into the garage. She'd ask him about it later.

That evening, she practiced her golf swing a little, then lay down on an outdoor chaise longue to read a book. She woke up just as the sun was setting, with the book resting on her chest.

Clearly, golf had done her in for the day. Abigail, who had been sleeping on the deck by her, suddenly jumped to her feet and started barking. She ran behind the cabin near the garage and barked hard at a man jogging down the road. He jumped when the dog came running, then realized how little the dog was. Waving at Carley, he kept on jogging. Carley waved back. It was the guy she had seen at the beach meeting and the golf course. She still couldn't recall who he was.

"What a big, ferocious dog you are!" Carley said to Abigail. She was glad that Abigail felt so territorial. Even if she wasn't much of a threat, at least she was a good alarm.

II

The young girl hid in the corner, afraid. She didn't know why she had been abducted. All she knew was that she was in a dank, windowless room with walls made of metal. She was chained to a large, heavy chair but had some room to move around. There was a stubby portable toilet designed for camping where she went to the bathroom. It had a lid, but even so, the smell was overpowering. And she had a blanket and a pillow to sleep on. That was it. At first, they'd kept her blindfolded with her arms tied behind her back. It was very uncomfortable, but she had learned how to position herself in the chair so it was tolerable. Now they had removed the blindfold and handcuffed her hands in front of her so she could eat. It was so dark, she couldn't see anything anyway. One of them sometimes came in to talk with her and give her a little treat. He seemed protective of her. He'd told her not to make too much noise, that he would do his best to keep her safe. She hoped he could.

She was sure she heard the men mention her stepfather. Did they know him? Was he involved? If it was money they were after, she would probably die there. Hal didn't have any. Neither did her mother, at least none that she knew about. She couldn't imagine any other reason they had kidnapped her. She shuddered. What would they do to her if they didn't get the money? She wished she knew if there was anyone else in the building or near the building, but she didn't dare scream; they had already told her they would kill her if she did. After feeling of the gun pointed between her ribs, she didn't want to find out if they were bluffing. While she had lost track of time, she was certain she had been there for days.

They brought her food—mostly cereal, chips, pizza once. She was glad to have something warm to eat. Well, it wasn't really warm, more room temperature. She figured she got their leftovers.

One of the men opened the door, lumbered over, and checked the chain that kept her tied to the chair. She could stand up; she just couldn't go anywhere without dragging the furniture with her. Taking her chin in his big hand, he asked, "So, how are you doing here all by yourself? Bet you're getting a little lonesome. How'd you like someone to keep you warm?" He smelled of liquor. She pulled away from him. His eyes flashing at her rejection, he gave the chair a push, and it went toppling over, pulling her with it. "Your dad had better make the right choices."

She shuddered, thinking of all the terrible things they might do to her. He wasn't her father, but she didn't want to tell this man anything. After the door clanged shut, she wrestled to get the chair upright. She thought her wrist was sprained, it hurt so much. Sprained or not, there was nothing she could do about it.

Straining to learn what she could about her surroundings, she could tell the floor was concrete and the walls were made of corrugated metal. After hearing the large garage-like door being locked and unlocked from the outside, she was certain it wasn't secured from the inside. Dragging the heavy chair with her, she had crawled all around the perimeter late at night, afraid they would hurt her if they found her trying to escape. It was a big, open room, about the size of the living room of their home. At night, it was cold. Hearing a little traffic off in the distance, she surmised they were on farmland, probably in a farm building. She hoped people were looking for her, but she never heard anyone outside calling her name. Why weren't they coming? Didn't anybody care?

She knew her mother did. She wasn't sure about Hal. They hadn't gotten along well since he'd married her mother. Maybe he had convinced her mother that she had run away. Would her mother believe him? She didn't know. It had been tough since Hal moved in with them. How did he know these men? How was he involved? How would she ever look him in the eye again? And would she ever have that chance?

12

It was the day of the golf tournament, and Carley was both excited and a little nervous about how she would do. When she arrived at the course, she learned she was paired with a threesome, two women and a man from Lake Melissa. They were very nice to her but were more interested in talking among themselves. The woman and man who were married jumped into a cart together. She rode in the cart with the other woman, the wife's sister. They were about fifteen years older than Carley, expert golfers who obviously hoped to win the cash prize. Not that it was a huge prize, but the thrill of winning seemed to spur them on.

By the end of the eighteen holes, she had learned that they were renting a cabin at the nearby lake, that they lived in Fargo, and that they golfed three or four times a week. Clearly, she was out of her league. In this best-ball tournament, they ended up using only two shots and one putt of hers. While she didn't expect to do much, this was even worse than she had feared. Bleak, actually. At the end of the tournament, they waved good-bye and parted company. Her hope of using golf to meet new friends was clearly dashed, at least for today.

As she left the clubhouse, she recognized the man Abigail startled as he was jogging by, the man she had seen at the driving range and the beach association meeting. He had a preoccupied look on his face as he lifted his clubs into the trunk of his car.

"Well," she said, "I hope you didn't embarrass yourself as much as I did!"

The man looked up from his bag and smiled. "Oh, I'm quite certain I brought up the rear."

She walked over to him and held out her hand. "Carley Norgren. I live in the log cabin with the terrier that tried to terrorize you yesterday."

"I thought I had seen you before. Mark Dolan. I'm staying in the yellow cabin a few doors down from you. Just renting for the summer," he said.

"I hope you're enjoying it. I love the lake," Carley said.

"It's really beautiful. I'm not from around here, so it's quite a nice surprise. A friend connected me with the person who owns the place where I'm staying."

"Where are you from?"

"Chicago."

"You're a long way from home, aren't you!" she exclaimed. She wondered how he ended up on Pelican but decided not to act too interested. "Well, I hope to see you again. Yell if my dog gets in your way!"

"Will do."

Okay, so if I just could meet one person every place I went, eventually I should end up with some friends, she thought. *One out of every ten would be a good return. One down, nine to go. God, it's hard starting over from scratch.*

* * *

When Carley got back to the cabin, she decided she needed some activities that didn't depend on anyone else. She'd always wanted to swim across the lake, about a two-mile stint. Eventually, she'd need someone to track her while she swam, but she could train by swimming along the lakeshore where it wasn't over her head. While she was a strong swimmer, she knew better than to get in too deep in a lake where boat waves and nonobservant jet skiers could prove dangerous. Trish would be that spotter for her. That would give her a month to lead up to the big event. In the meantime, she could practice swimming to the point and back, about a mile.

After changing into her swimsuit, she tethered Abigail to a tree and brought her towel down on the dock. The air had a little chill in it, and she didn't want to lose her nerve. Gracefully, she dove off the end of the dock and began swimming to the point, gliding over the surface. The water was a shock, but she quickly acclimated to the temperature. She could hear Abigail barking from the yard. Abigail always wanted to "save" her when she went swimming. Finally, the little dog's distress faded into the background. The rhythm of her breathing helped her move into a semiconscious dream state. Images flashed through her head—images of Mac, of her coworkers, of the golfers. No conclusions, no judgments—only a stream of consciousness. Letting go. It wasn't unpleasant, even though thinking of Mac usually sent her reeling. She felt sleek in the water. Years ago, she had competed on her high school's swim team.

By the time she made it to the point, she realized that her recent lack of exercise was catching up with her. She was winded; her muscles were already tired, and she had as far to go as she had already swum. She stood in the water and rested for a while. When she caught her breath, she started back toward her cabin. Partway there, she knew she couldn't make it. She swam to the shore and climbed out of the water. Ha—she wouldn't be able to do that when she was partway across the lake. It was still a couple of blocks to her home. She walked along the beach, climbing up and over people's docks. Even that took more energy than she had, so she walked along the edge of the properties leading back to her home. She felt a little self-conscious, though hardly anyone was there.

When she returned to her home, Abigail was resting comfortably under the tree, forgetting she was worried about Carley drowning. Carley, grabbing her towel and Abigail's leash, went back into the cabin, where Prattle was sound asleep, resting on one foot with the other tucked under her wing.

The man with the binoculars followed her trek into the house until she was no longer visible.

13

It was Wednesday morning, and Carley had no plans. Absent-mindedly, she picked up the paper. There wasn't much more about Lindsey, for which she was relieved. She wanted to read some good news for a change, though that was unlikely. Papers didn't make money by publishing good news. She kept hoping they'd find Lindsey hanging out somewhere with friends, but all her friends had come forward saying they didn't know where she was. Most of the headlines were about the drug problem flowing from Chicago to the oil pipelines in western North Dakota. It was a different environment from what she'd experienced in Fargo, living there in the '80s and '90s. She was grateful she had grown up in a simpler time.

She was leisurely drinking a cup of coffee when a cobalt-blue Maserati drove up the driveway to her cabin. Not recognizing it, she was curious about its driver. Out stepped a man, about her age, classically good looking, truly tall, dark, and handsome, looking like he had just come from a country club.

As she walked up to greet him, he held out his hand and offered her his business card. He removed the toothpick from his mouth and said, smiling apologetically and showing impressive dimples, "I'm sorry, I tried to call first, but your number isn't listed anywhere I could find. My name is Gordon Locklear. Are you Carley Norgren?"

"Yes, I am. Why?"

"I'm an associate professor in the chemistry department at the university. As a young assistant professor, I worked under your father, who was a mentor to me. He was someone I really admired, and he had a major influence on my professional career. I'm so glad to meet you."

"Wow! It's very nice to meet you too, Dr. Locklear." She assumed he had a PhD, since all the faculty in the department did.

"Please, call me Gordon."

"What are you doing here? Are you just passing by?"

"No, I came here to meet you."

"Really? Then today must be my lucky day," Carley said, raising an eyebrow.

"I have a special request. I've been working on a big project that builds on the work your father did. The research files of his work at the university are very incomplete. I wondered if you might have any of his records, and if you do, could I bring them back to the university?"

Carley was thrilled to have the chance to talk to someone who knew her father. She was surprised she hadn't met Gordon at her father's funeral. The university faculty and administration had turned out in droves, and this man would have stood out; surely, she would have noticed him.

He saw the look of puzzlement on her face and asked, "What's the matter?"

Sheepishly, she said, "I know this sounds presumptuous, but I'm surprised we're just meeting now, given how important my father was to you."

"I totally understand. I was shocked to learn of your father's death. At the time, I was in Europe working on a special NATO project in the Czech Republic. I couldn't leave the country in time for your father's funeral. I am so glad I have the chance to meet you now. If you're interested, I could share stories with you about your father sometime."

"I'd love to do that. That would be great."

"So, do you have any of his records?"

"I do. There is a whole file cabinet of them in the garage. I don't really know what all is in there. I've never gone through it."

"I'd be happy to help you sort that out," Gordon replied.

"Let me talk to my attorney. There may be records I need to keep for the patents or for future research."

"Fine. Why don't you give me a call after you've had a chance to check it out?"

"I will. It's really great meeting you. I'll look forward to the chance to talk more."

After he left, she took his card and went online. Yes, there was a Gordon Locklear listed as an associate professor at the university. The website indicated his PhD was from the university of Minnesota and listed the classes he taught and articles he published. She was disappointed there were no pictures of any of the faculty except group shots. She didn't spot Gordon in any of those. Her father was still in one of the pictures; they hadn't removed it from the department website.

She didn't know how valuable her father's files were, but she felt odd just turning them over to someone else. She would contact her attorney to get his advice. Of course, she hoped she would see Gordon again. It was comforting to talk with someone who knew her father. It felt like a voice from the past reaching out to her. And he was good looking. That didn't hurt. But while she wanted to help him out, she also had to be smart about what she was doing.

* * *

That afternoon, Carley called her attorney to see what he suggested. He advised her that, while it was her choice, she should only allow copies of the files to be removed from the premises. His biggest concern was that others from the university might claim the work as their own and that the university might try to claim ownership of the documents. He suggested she have Gordon Locklear sign a nondisclosure agreement to protect the information, agreeing that he would not distribute the information in any way without her permission. He would have to get her approval before any further applications of her father's research could be developed. The attorney said he would e-mail Carley forms that would protect her father's—and ultimately her—interests. It would also give her the chance to review enhancements to her father's work with the chair of the department. In many ways, she thought this was above and beyond what was necessary, but lawyers were like that. Since she would never be able to use her father's research herself, she didn't have a problem sharing it with his protégé, but she would do what her attorney suggested. The biggest problem, it seemed to her, was that there was no photocopier at her cabin.

She called Gordon back and told him she would be happy to give him the opportunity to see and use her father's files. She also explained that she had been advised by her attorney to only allow photocopies to be removed from the premises. That meant Gordon would have to get equipment set up in the garage that would allow him to make copies. She would review the copies to be sure she knew what he was taking.

Gordon was visibly excited and grateful. He said he completely understood the attorney's reservations and would arrange for a photocopier. He asked if there were outlets in the garage. Carley indicated there were. In the meantime, he wondered if she would join him for dinner at a great restaurant outside of Vergas so they could talk about how they would work these arrangements out. He would pick her up around 5:00 that evening. She had heard of the restaurant, though she hadn't been there since it opened a year and a half earlier.

When she hung up, she realized she felt a little bubble rising in her stomach. She was attracted to him. He was the first man since Mac who had caught her attention, and his relationship with her father was decidedly a plus. If nothing else, she would learn more about her father's work, and that was exciting in and of itself.

* * *

Dinner that evening was lively. She wore a brightly flowered sundress that was part of her favorite lake attire. It was unusual for her to be out of her swimsuit or khaki shorts, so it was the sundress or jeans. The restaurant was very rustic—a log cabin with a beautiful interior and view of a lake.

Gordon said, "I feel very lucky to be in such a beautiful place with such a wonderful woman."

Carley blushed. "It's not every day I get transported in such fine style."

"I'm glad you like my car."

She said, "I do, but can I ask you a really bold question?"

"Sure," he responded. "Shoot."

"How can you afford such a fancy sports car on a professor's salary? I have an idea of how much a professor makes, and I know my dad couldn't have afforded one."

He laughed sheepishly. "The money for the car came from an inheritance from my grandfather. Because we shared a love of sports cars, I felt my grandfather would approve."

Nice, she thought.

They talked animatedly throughout the evening. Clearly, there was a mutual spark.

"Your dad was one of the most dedicated men I've ever met," Gordon stated. "He worked twelve to fourteen hours a day, never complaining. Most faculty don't work that hard, but your father had an open-door policy for students. Someone was always stopping by to ask for his help. Students loved him. So did his peers."

Carley became quiet for a moment, then asked, "So, what's your favorite memory of my father?"

Gordon replied, "That's easy. It was how fairly he always dealt with everyone. He would never compromise his principles, no matter how much he liked someone."

"What was his relationship with Hal?"

Gordon became pensive. "I don't know. They didn't seem that close."

"How about you and Hal?" she asked.

"Well, we get along fine. I don't know. We're different people. We're competitive in some ways. I feel sorry for what he's going through right now. Let's talk about something else," he suggested.

They went on to talk about the lake, his childhood, her childhood, what her father was like as a father, what their dream vacations were. No subject was off limits.

When he brought her back to her cabin that evening, he brought her to the door and kissed her gently. The kiss caused a stirring Carley hadn't expected. As she watched him drive off, waves of both apprehension and giddiness overpowered her. She didn't want to fall for anyone. Certainly not yet. Not now. Did she?

14

Late the next morning, Gordon arrived with a long power cord, a printer/copier, a couple of freshly glazed doughnuts, and coffee for both of them. Carley was impressed by his thoughtfulness, even though the coffee was now only lukewarm. The coffee shop was, of course, about twenty minutes away. She asked him how long he thought it would take to review the files, and he estimated at least four or five days. Secretly, she was glad. It felt good to have someone else around.

She told him she'd be working on the garden; he should just let her know what he needed.

About two hours later, Gordon came out of the garage to stretch. He had several papers in his hands and showed her the copies he wanted to take. She looked the papers over, wishing she knew anything at all about what they contained. It was all Greek to her, mostly very technical papers with formulas and diagrams. He asked if she'd like to go into town and have lunch with him, and she said yes immediately.

Riding in the Maserati was exhilarating. He offered to let her drive it. Because it had a stick shift, Carley was afraid at first she'd kill the engine. However, it was just like riding a bicycle. Soon they were zipping past corn fields and farmland, taking back roads void of speed traps and patrol cars. Carley grinned as she maneuvered skillfully around curves and hills. Gordon was clearly amused by how much fun she was having. They found a little restaurant on the Pelican River—very scenic, not very expensive, overlooking the water, and "the largest Pelican in the world," a twenty-foot statue the town was known for.

Lunch provided very animated conversation. They exchanged stories about life in a small town, about life at the university, and life in a corporate buyout.

"Would you tell me a little about my father's research?" Carley asked. "My dad always tried to get me interested in science, but I just wasn't. Now I wish I knew more about his work."

"Sure. I'll give you the short version right now. If you want, I can even give you a couple of academic papers he wrote. They're fairly complex. I'm glad your father was there to explain all of it to me!"

He picked up the glass of soda in front of him. "See this? Let's say I wanted to find out the chemical makeup of this liquid. When light hits any element, there is a shift in the light. Each element has its own chemical fingerprint, so each element will shift the light in a different way. A spectrometer is a device that can determine the composition of any element by calculating how it changes the light. I know it sounds complicated, but it's exciting stuff. Typically, every research university could only afford one spectrometer, because they cost several hundred thousand dollars. Also, they take up an entire room and must have their own air-conditioning. Your dad developed a handheld device that would do the same thing and cost a fraction of what the others cost, probably closer to $25,000."

"What would you want to use this for?"

"There are so many applications! It can be used in water treatment plants to identify what metals and contaminates are in the water. It can be used in transportation to scan shipments. It can be used in astronomy to test samples brought from space. Any time someone needs to understand what an element is made of, this device is useful. It has endless applications. Plus, the portability of the spectrometer your father developed means that even small colleges can purchase one for their chemistry and physics labs. That, in itself, is huge. And he found a way to measure 'dark' substances that couldn't be identified in a spectrometer before, like black tar heroin and black explosives, like gun powder."

"Where do you want to take his research now?"

"There are many directions it could go. I've been thinking about its applications in farming, since that's the biggest industry around this area."

"That's sounds like something my father would be interested in," Carley remarked. "I'd really appreciate you showing me some of the papers and what you're learning from them. I am interested in learning more."

"Not a problem. I'd enjoy doing that," Gordon said, placing his hand on her knee.

Near the end of their meal, Gordon pointed to a sign out the window that read Kayaks for Rent and said to Carley, with a twinkle in his eyes, "What do you think? Are you game?"

"I'm game. Can you spare the time?" Carley asked.

"I can if you can," he responded with a smile revealing his dimples. "After all, I'm a professor, and it's summer. I don't have a schedule to keep."

After lunch, they had the outfitter drop them off upstream on the river, and they kayaked back into town. It was a gorgeous day, and they had fun bantering with each other all the way down the river. It wasn't a challenging course, and they reached town about an hour and a half later.

"I haven't laughed that much in a long time," Gordon said with a grin.

"Me, neither," admitted Carley. The chemistry between them was palpable. She felt relaxed with him, intrigued by him.

"Let's go back, and I'll work on those files another couple of hours and then call it a day," he suggested.

* * *

The rest of the afternoon sped by, and by 5:30, Gordon was on his way. When he left, he thanked Carley and told her he would be back the next day around 10:00 in the morning if that worked for her. It did. He also asked her if she'd like to have dinner some night soon. He had heard about a great restaurant in Dilworth, a nearby town, and thought it might be fun to check out. She agreed. He looked into her eyes in a way that made her blush. Gently, he cupped her chin in his hands. Leaning in to her, he gave her a tender kiss.

As she walked back into the cabin, she marveled at how quickly he had entered her life and thoughts. She really liked him—he was confident but not cocky, bright but not overbearing, and genuinely fun to be with. It mattered a great deal that he had known and cared about her father. She could see why her father had mentored him. She didn't have the chance to talk about her father very often, so it had been especially fun to hear the new stories Gordon shared. He told her small things about her father that she had never known, especially about things at work, conferences where he was the keynote speaker, awards he had won. It made her both happy and sad to hear more about his professional life. It amazed her that her father never talked about any of that at home, at least not in front of her. She wished she had heard her father talk about Gordon. It would be fun to know what he thought of him. They had a bond she didn't even know about. While that didn't bother her, she realized how much she didn't know about her dad.

* * *

The next day, Gordon showed up bright and early with two lukewarm coffees. When Carley came out of the cabin to greet him, he gave her a hug. "What a great surprise it's been to meet you," he said as he pulled her closer to him. "I thought I was coming here to get ahold of some exciting research. I didn't know I'd meet someone equally exciting!"

She grinned, feeling that same small bubble rise inside her. It was as if her father had brought them together. The thought was a little startling. Was that why she felt so attracted to him?

"How about that dinner?" he asked with a smile.

"I'd love to," she responded. "Tonight?"

"Sure. Why not?" he asked. "It's a great place—the best steak around. That'll give us a chance to get to know each other a little better."

"Well, let's go," she said. She realized it had been awhile since she'd felt this carefree or this pursued. It was nice, though a little niggling voice told her not to move too fast.

"Back to the salt mines," he quipped. With that, he kissed her sweetly and headed for the garage.

About an hour and a half later, she brought some freshly made lemonade to the garage. He looked up at her appreciatively. It was hot in the garage, but he had been so absorbed in what he was doing he had hardly noticed.

"Why don't you take a break? We could go sit on the end of the dock and enjoy this beautiful day," she offered.

Smiling, he said, "That would be great. Let's do it."

They spent the next hour dangling their feet in the water, talking about university politics, her father, the sunfish that were nipping at their toes, what her next career steps might be. He pulled her toward him, kissing her on the top of her head. She leaned into him. He tipped her head toward him and placed a gentle, lingering kiss on her lips. She felt a current run through her body.

As he wrapped both arms around her, he said, "Why did it take us so long to meet?"

Surprised that he was asking the same question she was thinking, she laughed.

"What's so funny?" he asked with a slightly hurt look in his eyes.

"That's just what I was wondering," she responded.

With that, he pulled her close to him and kissed her hard. She drew in a quick breath and then kissed him with an intensity that surprised her. As they leaned together, suddenly Gordon lost his balance and slid off the dock into the cold lake water. "Oh no. If I'm in here, you're coming too." Quickly he grabbed her by the arm and pulled her into the water on top of him before she had a chance to protest. They both stood up in the chest-high water, laughing and chortling, while Abigail barked and Prattle began to chirp up in the cabin. He pulled her toward him as he swam on his back. She was such a strong swimmer that she broke free and dunked him under the water. He reciprocated, and soon they were in an all-out water war.

He raised up his arms and said, "I give!"

She laughed, and he put his arm around her as they climbed out of the water onto the shore. Carley sprinted into the cabin to find them both towels. Prattle, excited by the activity, paced back and forth agitatedly across her perch. "You're okay, Prattle. We're just having a little fun."

They both dried off, but their clothes were drenched, and the sun was low in the sky. "Some of my brother's clothes might fit you. Want to try?"

"Sure. I'll take anything."

She ran to her brother's bedroom and found some sweat pants and a sweatshirt. They were a little musty smelling—they hadn't been used for several years—but at least they were dry.

When she returned, she handed him the clothes. As he reached for them, he took her by the arm, pulled her close to him, and kissed her. She leaned into the kiss, knowing this day was the start of something big.

15

Although Gordon had to stay in Fargo for a couple of days, he told Carley he would come back on Thursday. It was Thursday now, and she awoke with a sense of anticipation. Her sundress called to her from her closet, and she put it on. Looking out the window, she saw Gordon, right on schedule, getting out of his sports car with two, probably lukewarm, coffees in hand. He had a little brown paper bag as well. She leaped down the stairs to see him. As she opened the door, a sly smile came across his face.

"We're going to eat our way through this relationship!" He laughed. "There's a new bakery in Fargo, and I couldn't resist their almond croissants. I hope you can't, either. I'd hate to eat alone." He offered up the brown paper bag to her.

Smiling, she accepted both the coffee and the croissant. "So, what's on the agenda today?" she asked.

"Well, more of the scintillating sifting through papers and copying, I assume. What did you have in mind?" he asked coyly.

"Why don't you work for a couple of hours and we can go into DL for lunch? There's a new brewery that just opened with a gourmet menu for lunch. Want to try it?"

"Sure. Will you wear that dress?" he asked with an irresistible smile.

Catching her breath, she said, "We could head over there about 11:30. So get busy!"

With that, Gordon gave her a slight bow and a rolling wave with his hand and headed to the garage.

Two hours later, they took off in his Maserati for Detroit Lakes. As they wound along the back roads, Carley marveled at the rural scenery—rolling green hills, lazy cows, old barns, rickety fences. "It would be fun to do this again and bring a camera," she commented.

Gordon smiled at her, grabbed her hand, and said, "That can be arranged!"

The brewery was indeed trendy, every bit as interesting as those in the Twin Cities. The food might even be better. They ordered beer samplers, gourmet burgers, fries with aioli. Their conversation ranged from childhood escapades to more current events in their lives. She shared how much she wanted to travel and that this might be the time in her life to take an extended trip she'd never had time to do before. They both hoped to visit New Zealand and some of the South Pacific islands like Tahiti and Fiji. It seemed uncanny how much they had in common.

Gordon put his hand over Carley's, gently stroking it. "I really like you," he said. "There isn't anyone else in my life, and there hasn't been for a while. I'm more than ready for a real relationship. How about you?"

She blanched as she thought about Mac. "Well, there isn't anyone in my life now. I just got out of a significant relationship. It's one of the reasons I'm up here. I don't want to get involved too fast, but I have to admit I find you intriguing too."

With that, he moved in closer and gave her a long, hard kiss on the lips. Smiling, he said, "Let's get out of here."

* * *

The ride back was a quieter one. When he wasn't shifting gears, Gordon kept his hand resting on hers. He looked at her often. She smiled back, unable to quite grasp how fast this was happening.

At the lake, Gordon jumped out of the car to open her door. She laughed at his chivalry.

"What?" he asked with a pretend hurt look.

"Sucking up, are we?" she asked with feigned innocence.

"I'd be happy to show you sucking up," he said, showing his dimples once again. With that, he drew her close and began kissing her slowly at first, then with more passion. His tongue found its way into her mouth, and again, she was surprised at how much she wanted him.

He reached down and ran his hands up her bare legs under her dress. He pulled back from her with a questioning look.

She laughed again. "If we're going to do this, we'd better go inside before I change my mind," she mused.

With that, Gordon swept her up into his arms and brought her into the cabin. Accidentally bumping her head on the woodwork as they entered, he rubbed it gently and said, "This isn't as easy as it looks in the movies." He set her on her feet and pulled her close.

She took his hand and headed toward the stairs. *Am I really doing this?* It was as if she were watching two other star-struck lovers making their way upstairs.

Once in the bedroom, he pulled her toward him and kissed her longingly, deeply. She responded with the same intensity. Gently, he pulled her sundress over her head. She reciprocated by removing his shirt. They both started laughing when it got caught on his head.

"It helps to unbutton all the buttons before you try that!" He laughed.

She felt out of practice, even though it hadn't been that long.

They resumed kissing with even more intensity, as if time were running out. She lay down on one of the twin beds, reaching out for his hand and pulling him toward her until they were locked in an embrace that kept them both from falling out of bed. As he touched her breasts, gliding his strong hand gently over them, she gasped. His hand followed around her back, gently stroking her back and buttocks. His mouth moved to her breast, and he gently slid his fingers to the most alive part of her body. Arching her back, her body began to move in sync with his. He knew just how to touch her. Her body felt like a tightly wound clock. The tension in her body building, it wouldn't take much to push her over the edge. Quickly it became too intense, and her body was overwhelmed by strong, wonderful contractions.

She reached for him, then gasped. What about protection? It hadn't crossed her mind. She'd been on the birth control pill for so long with Mac, she forgot it couldn't be that spontaneous.

It was as if he read her mind. "Was this what you were thinking about?" he said as he reached for a condom in his pants pocket. "I was hoping I'd get lucky!" He raised his eyebrows, acknowledging what was about to happen.

Carley laughed and exhaled. Pulling him back close to her, they started moving together again. She stared into his eyes as she guided him into her. It didn't take long until he was moving with rhythm, faster and faster, pushing deeper and deeper into her until he exploded inside her. They both fell back on the bed, breathless and totally spent. After a little time, she rolled carefully off the bed, walked over by the other twin bed, and pushed the two together. He jumped to his feet to help her. As they slid under the light covers, she nestled up tightly against him, and he wrapped his broad arms around her. She felt content, satisfied in a way she hadn't felt for a long, long time.

"I've been wanting to do that ever since we met," Gordon said. She had to admit she had too. After they had lain there some time, he gently climbed out of bed, put on his pants, and gave her a sweet kiss on her lips. "See you tomorrow," he said.

16

The next morning, as she lay in bed stretching, she couldn't stop a small, slow smile from creeping across her face. She felt a newfound sense of optimism, and yet, if she were honest with herself, that feeling made her uneasy. Something about all this was too good to be true, and in her life experience, that usually meant it was. She could see a warning flag on the horizon, yet she was quite sure she would ignore it until it was a little closer. Or perhaps a neon color. She chuckled to herself. For now, Gordon was interesting. Smart, good looking, affectionate. Still, things were moving very fast, faster than she normally would have let them.

A knock at the back door broke her reverie. She slipped into a well-loved terry cloth robe and headed to the door. Abigail was barking agitatedly until the voice on the other side said, "Good doggie. Good doggie. Have you forgotten me already, Abigail?"

Carley opened the door and feigned a look of disgust at Gordon, who was standing on the step, juggling two cups of coffee, a bag of sweet rolls, a small bag of dog bones, and his briefcase. "So now you're bribing her too?" Carley queried.

"It never hurts to have a dog on your side," Gordon retorted. He handed her the coffee cups, set down his briefcase, and gave her a tender kiss. "What's on your agenda for the day?"

"I have two specification sheets I have to get done for my marketing VP today, then I'm a free woman," Carley said. "How about you?"

"I have a file I want to get through today, and then I'd love to take a break."

"Do you like to fish?" she asked.

"Hmmmm . . . I might. I don't know. I haven't tried it much. How about going for a sailboat ride instead?"

"You're on," she said.

With that, Gordon disappeared into to the garage, and Carley disappeared upstairs with her coffee and papers.

Hours later, Gordon and Carley headed over to the Pelican Lake Yacht Club to pick up the boat they had reserved. There were no races today since it was a weekday, so they had their choice of boats. They chose a thirteen-foot Enterprise that would allow them to both sail fast and lollygag.

They tacked to the other side of the lake and set the sail for a leisurely pace down the lake. Combined, their expertise made it easy to manage the boat. It was a day with bright blue skies and just enough wind. Popping open a couple of bottles of beer, they nestled into comfortable positions in the boat. There wasn't much traffic on the lake, so they wouldn't have to do aggressive steering.

"Tell me more about your work," Gordon encouraged Carley. "You're a consultant? Do you like that?"

"You know, I love the independence way more than I'd expected to. If I had a long-term contract, it could be very exciting to be a consultant, but if I always have to worry about where work is coming from, that would be more challenging. We'll see. I'm thinking about staying in the area no matter what."

Gordon looked pleased by that comment. "Good. Fargo isn't that far away."

She was pleasantly surprised by his reaction. "What about you? Tell me about the university. What do you like best about being there?"

"You know, it's a stimulating environment. It was better when your dad was there. He was such a great leader for our department. It just isn't much money, you know?"

As the breeze died down, their conversation lulled as well. They leaned into each other, pulling each other closer. As gentle waves lapped up against the sailboat, their kissing became more passionate. Soon their bodies were moving in the same rhythm as the water.

When he left that evening, he kissed her tenderly and told her he'd be back in a couple of days. He had some paperwork he needed to catch up on, but he would be back. She knew he would.

17

Two days later, Gordon arrived as planned, at 10:00 a.m. on the nose. Carley was glad to see him. It felt right having him there. While he was tending to the files in the garage, she cleaned the gutters, which clearly hadn't had attention for several years. Abigail, who was tethered, strained to be as close to her as she could. Carley adjusted the wheelbarrow, moved the ladder, and started digging wet leaves, acorns, and dirt out of the gutter. It was hard work, but hard work never fazed her.

"Well, I think I'm done," he announced. "Can you believe I'm finished?"

Carley was caught off guard. She was up on the ladder, elbow deep in filth. "Just a second—I'll be right down," she said as she peeled off the rubber gloves. "Did you find everything you needed?"

"Yes, it was very helpful. Here—I know you want to see what I copied." He handed her a small stack of research notes, none of which made any sense to Carley. "Most of it is the result of product testing and what your dad found, especially in developing the prototype for manufacturing. He had identified some alternative ways of structuring the spectrometer that could make it much easier to use. That's where my research will pick up."

"That's great." She nodded, not fully understanding how he planned to use the information he had. She trusted him, though.

"Sometime, we should get together with the dean and talk through the implications of using my dad's research. My attorney is interested in being part of a discussion like that. I don't know what it all means, but it would helpful to understand where my father's work ends and the university's and yours begins."

Gordon said, "I understand. I'd be happy to set that meeting up. I've got a lot of work to do now that I have the missing pieces of information. Next week, I'll be at an academic conference in Colorado on spectrometry, and I'll be gone about a week and a half. If I'd known you sooner, I'd have asked you to come along. We've been advised we won't have much cell phone coverage at the mountain resort where the conference is being held, but I'll call you as soon as I get back. There's a special place I'd like to take you for dinner. It's about a forty-five-minute drive from here in the most romantic setting I know. And we can get the meeting with the dean on the calendar too."

Smiling, he pulled her toward him. "It's really been great getting to know you in so many ways. I can't wait to get to know you better. There is so much I want to do and see with you."

"I agree," she added. "Yes, I'd really like that." She was a little sad he hadn't invited her to go along. She was up for almost any kind of adventure, even though she knew that was about the last thing she needed in her life right now. Plus, she didn't have anyone to care for her pets, so it was totally ludicrous for her to even think it might work.

Gordon gave her a long, hard kiss. "I'll call you as soon as I'm back," he said.

* * *

After Gordon left, Carley sat down on an old tree stump, feeling slightly dazed. She hadn't expected him to leave quite so early that morning or quite so suddenly, though she had known he was almost done with his work. Ten days felt like a long time to go without any conversation, but she was certain he'd call if he could find a way. Wouldn't a resort have access to the Internet, even if cell phone coverage was uncertain? Maybe it was just her lonesomeness talking, but she knew she could really fall for this man. If she were honest with herself, she already had.

* * *

The next morning when she awoke, Carley felt energized and ready for work. She fed Abigail, let her out without tethering her, and sat back down for a cup of hazelnut coffee. She picked up the paper from the day before, which she hadn't yet read, and mindlessly skimmed articles about a crew stranded in a mine shaft in the western part of North Dakota, predictions of a deficit for the state budget, and an announcement about the new CEO of the snowmobile manufacturing company in Fargo. She started working on the sudoku puzzle. Suddenly, she realized she hadn't let Abigail back in the house. Carley opened the door, but Abigail was nowhere to be seen. It was very unlike her; she was so tuned in to Carley, she rarely left her immediate vicinity. Carley, still in her pajamas, didn't want to go on a hunt for her dog. However, within minutes, she had slipped into her jeans and put a baseball cap over her hair. She jogged out to the road and looked both directions. She couldn't see any sign of Abigail, so she veered off to the left.

She called, but there was no sight of Abigail. She continued down the road, stopping to call every fifty feet or so, hoping Abigail hadn't chased something into the woods that bordered the road. When she reached the end of the beach, she turned and went back the way she had come. She continued jogging past her cabin. Still no Abigail. She called as loudly as she could. It was so unlike the dog, it made her nervous. Could an eagle have swooped her up? It seemed unlikely; fish and small rodents were so prevalent there was no need to pick up an animal as large as Abigail. Had someone taken her? She continued calling. She jogged out to the road, past the stop sign, past the truck junkyard near the storage units. This seemed much farther than Abigail's little legs could carry her. Turning back, she called and called. Suddenly she heard a muffled, mewing sound and stopped to see if she could determine where the noise was coming from. It must be a cat in the tall grass or some other small animal. It didn't sound like Abigail. She listened closely but couldn't hear the noise any longer.

She saw Ben ambling back to his cabin and called out to him, "Hey, Ben! Did you see Abigail since you've been out walking?"

Ben shook his head. "Nope. Haven't seen your dog today."

As she approached her cabin, Abigail came running out to greet her. The dog was filthy; she looked like she had been rolling in oil. She seemed fine, however, and panted excitedly when Carley picked her up and hugged her.

"Don't do that again, Abigail," Carley warned. "You scared me."

As she looked around, Carley was stunned to find the door to the garage open. She knew the door wasn't open when she left, or she would have looked there first for Abigail. Hadn't she shut the new lock she'd put on? And where was the lock now? She peered into the dark garage and reached for the chain to turn on the light. Looking down, she saw that an oil can had been knocked over. So, Abigail really had been rolling in oil.

Oh, great, Carley thought. Then her mind went somewhere more sinister. Who was interested in her garage? And why? From what she could tell, the garage had been broken into three times just since she'd been there. What was going on? Ben had been in the area. Did he have anything to do with it? As she looked around, she couldn't see anything missing. She spread some cat litter her dad had kept in the garage just for that purpose over the oil. What did someone think was so valuable in there? She chuckled. It reminded her of the time someone tried to break into their garage years ago and ended up breaking into the old outhouse on the side of the garage instead. What a surprise that must have been.

Carley thought about calling the police to let them know her garage had been broken into again. Then she tried to picture their response, especially if she was unsure whether anything had been taken. They had more important matters to deal with, she knew. Plus, they'd already been out to check her garage once before. The break-ins made her feel violated, nervous. She realized it was her own unease, not a crime, that was prevailing. She didn't make the call.

18

The young girl shivered while the man held the gun to her head. She had heard someone calling, "Abigail." Though that wasn't her name, she hoped that someone might hear her. When she heard the calls, she tried mewing back, hoping she would be heard. Unfortunately, one of her captors heard her first. He immediately charged into the space where she was being held and put the gun to her head. If only someone outside had heard her. Would it matter? Would anyone ever find her? She was beginning to give up hope.

19

Carley picked up the paper and saw that there was a barbecue, band, and salsa dancing that night on the other end of the lake at a public landing, sponsored by the lake association. She recalled getting an e-mail announcement of the event too. She was sure she would see someone there she would know. If not, perhaps she could make a new friend or two. Gordon had left for the conference, and this was a nice chance for her to venture out alone.

Feeling very energetic, she plowed through her work on the product release. It was taking shape, and she had a strategy that she thought would be effective. She needed to flesh it out further so she could review it with their industrial advisory panel.

She was also beginning to have a sense of structure to her life at the lake. Always feeling like she was on vacation had pitfalls. As one day merged into the next, she had needed something to give her a little more sense of normalcy. Starting each day with a swim gave her that reason to get up. She could feel herself getting stronger. Every day she did something that got her out of the cabin; tonight, it would be dancing. For the second time in a month, she put on makeup.

When she arrived at the event, she was pleased to see some of her neighbors whom she recognized. They had a large table and invited her to join their group. While she didn't know them well, she had a sense of comfort knowing they were there. She didn't see many people from high school, and for that she was relieved.

When the dancing started, her neighbors pulled her out onto the dance floor with them. The dance floor was really an asphalt parking lot, but it was such a fun, low-key event, it didn't matter.

Another man joined their group as the neighbors waved him in. She was surprised to see Mark again, or at least surprised that he was already such a hit with the neighbors. He was a fun, outgoing, athletic person, it was true, and the neighbors seemed to know him and enjoy him. She wondered how he'd gotten to know everyone so fast when he was much more of an outsider than she was. She felt an annoying twinge of jealousy that she didn't want to admit.

The dancing was fast and energetic. At one point, having tripped over her own two feet one too many times, Carley decided to sit the next song out. She went back to the table and soon was joined by Mark, who seemed equally done in.

"I haven't done that much bad dancing in a long time," quipped Mark.

Carley laughed. She thought he looked fine dancing and told him so. She had decided years earlier that, even though she would never be a great dancer, the people she admired most on the dance floor didn't hold back, even if they didn't have the best moves. Having fun was all that mattered in the end.

"Can I buy you a drink?" he asked.

She nodded. "Gin and tonic."

When he returned with their drinks, he asked, "So, what brings you up to this nirvana?"

She told him her history at the lake and about the company buyout. She omitted the parts about Mac and having to move out under duress. *Jobless, loveless,* and *homeless* were not great conversation starters.

"Now it's your turn. What brings you here from Chicago? I would think there would be a lot of lakes between here and there."

Mark hesitated. "Well, I'm not really here on vacation. I'm a rep for the construction firm for the condominiums being planned in Fish Lake. I'm working on the legal aspects and some of the lake requirements for building in a protected area."

Carley despised the condominium project, which was going to change the landscape of the lake, but she decided not to mention that right now. The project was very controversial, and, after all, she was just getting to know him.

Mark continued, "How would you like to do something sometime? The neighbors here are friendly and have included me in some of the beach events, but the truth is, overall, the summer has been pretty dull."

She said, "Sure," even though she wasn't sure at all. She knew nothing about him and suspected he had a significant other. If he didn't, she wasn't really interested in becoming one. Even though he was growing on her, she could only focus on one man in her life at a time, and Gordon had her full attention.

"I've been thinking about rebuilding part of my lake home," Carley volunteered. "Perhaps you could help me figure out how much it will cost to do what I want."

"Certainly willing to try," he said. "I probably won't know, but I know people who can help. I'm not involved in that end of the business—I work on any legal complications that arise—but I have connections."

After they finished their drinks, they went back out onto the dance floor to learn some new salsa moves. Mark grabbed her and spun her off the dance floor. She started to lose her balance, but Mark caught her just as she stumbled. She laughed as he grabbed her, and soon they were both chortling as they staggered off to the side of the dance floor.

Mark pulled her close to him and gave her a hug. The hug caught her off guard. It wasn't bad—she was just surprised. Instinctively, she flinched. It had been a great night. She didn't want to give him the wrong impression. He was a nice guy; she just wasn't interested in anything more.

20

Her cell phone was jangling. It was 7:00 a.m., and it woke her from a deep reverie. She answered groggily, "Hullo?"

Much to her shock, it was Mac. She hadn't focused her eyes enough to see who was calling. If she had, she would have let it roll over into voice mail.

"Hi. It's me. Mac," he said unceremoniously. "How are you?"

Her mouth was dry, and her heart leaped into her throat. She could hardly talk. "Fine."

"I was looking for something and found a few boxes of yours in the storage closet, piled up behind some plastic crates. I thought you might need them."

Her mind was swirling. "I haven't had time to miss much of anything yet. I've already brought so much stuff up here," she replied. "I have no idea what's in those boxes, but I suppose you'd like me to take them off your hands."

"No rush. I just wanted to let you know the boxes were here. If you want me to open them and see what's in there, I'm happy to do that."

"That's all right. So, do you want to ship them to me?"

"No, I'll figure out something else. A couple of them are quite heavy. Probably books. I'll just hang on to them until I have an easy way to get them to you, if that's all right with you. How are things at the lake?"

By now, she was sitting upright, trying to shake off her sleepiness. That wasn't hard. She felt like she had been electrocuted.

"They're good." She didn't want to share too much with him. "How are you?" She was quite sure he was doing fine, or he would have waited until evening to call her.

"Work is going well; life is good. Our softball team is number one in the league," he said. Well, it used to be *their* softball team. Now it was the team he and his new friend played on. It was an awkward conversation. Carley could feel her heart pounding and she was struggling to sound coherent.

"Well, thanks for letting me know about the boxes."

"Sure. I really hope you're doing well. You take care," he concluded.

She couldn't shake the terrible feeling she had after talking with Mac. How long would it take before the sound of his voice didn't send her into a deep, dark valley? She got dressed and drank a glass of juice. Abigail was begging to go out, so Carley put on her running shoes, grabbed the leash, and headed out the door. She fell into a smooth, comfortable run. It was therapeutic for her. Abigail had to run at full tilt to keep up with her. Finally, Carley settled into a brisk walk so Abigail could catch her breath. As they walked past the cabin Mark was renting, Abigail saw him and immediately started barking.

"Ha!" Carley said. "I brought my attack dog with me."

Mark looked startled. He was loading equipment into his car and didn't seem to expect anyone to be around so early. He appeared uncomfortable, and Carley was instantly sorry she had walked by his cabin.

"We'll give you a little peace and quiet," she said, scooping Abigail into her arms. She was glad she wasn't interested in him or she would have been greatly discouraged. She couldn't figure out exactly why she wasn't. He was good looking, a little older than Gordon—probably in his late thirties, maybe even early forties. He was not as tall as Gordon—or Mac, for that matter. Did height matter to her? As a volleyball player, she was used to being around "tall trees." She was one of the shorter players she knew and, at five foot eight, wasn't really short. No, it had to be something more than height, she mused. He was so earnest—too serious, perhaps. She liked someone with a little more spice. Or was that what always got her into trouble?

She continued walking down the road at a brisk pace for another forty-five minutes. When they returned home, Abigail was panting hard. Carley checked her e-mail and saw an announcement that a second search was being organized for Hal's stepdaughter. She wanted to help, although she questioned whether a search would do any good. There was no trail, meaning she willingly got into a vehicle or was forced into one and taken away from the area. While she doubted that a search could be successful, she wanted to support Hal. Even though he was the lead suspect, she couldn't believe that such a fundamentally good person could do something so despicable.

The search would start the next morning. Today, she was looking forward to kicking back. She was waiting for the VP to respond to her marketing plan, she'd cut the grass earlier, she had all the groceries she needed. Now she could just relax.

Suddenly, there was a knock on the door. Much to her surprise, it was Mark.

"Hi there. I came by for two reasons. One is to say I'm sorry. I didn't mean to blow you off this morning. I just had a lot on my mind. The other was to ask if you'd like to go for a quick run. I need to clear my head, and that always seems to work."

She agreed, and off they went. She left Abigail behind because she was quite sure the little dog wouldn't be able to keep up. The dog moped as she watched Carley go down the path.

They ran a couple of miles and ended back at his place, jumping into the water. It felt good. He brought out a couple of beach towels. As they sat there, he asked her questions about what had brought her back to the lake, why it was such a special place to her. He asked about her father, saying he'd heard such good things about him. She was surprised by that, but he said the neighbors raved about him one night. She explained he was a chemical engineer who'd taught at the state university in Fargo. He wasn't the stereotypical researcher; he was a very warm and personable man. She supposed that was pigeonholing researchers. He asked her what kind of research her father had been involved in. She told him it was very complex. Her father held thirty-two patents. Some of them had to do with fission, some with chemical reactions, and some with spectrometry. He used to take her to his laboratory and let her see what he was working on. He asked if her father knew Hal. She said everyone knew almost everyone in Fargo. Both men worked in the same department at the university, though Hal was much more junior. Her father had offered to mentor Hal, but she didn't think that had really happened. That shifted the conversation to the missing girl and the search the next day.

"Why don't you come with me?" she asked.

"I'll think about it. I don't have any meetings tomorrow, so maybe I can," he responded. "What about your friend? I've noticed you've had a lot of company lately."

Carley flushed. It really wasn't his business. She said, "He used to work with my father and asked if he could come and review his files because it turns out the university doesn't have complete sets of his patents or the new work he had undertaken just before he died." She wasn't about to tell him she was interested in Gordon.

She decided it was time to leave. The conversation had made her uneasy, though she didn't know why. Perhaps it was because the thought of the missing girl was just too much for her. Mark was nice enough, but something about him made her a little uncomfortable.

21

The three men huddled in the storage shed to plan their next steps. They had heard about the search efforts and were worried. They knew that Lindsey had tried to communicate with someone who was near the storage shed. She was clever, not calling out but making a noise that could draw someone closer. A pistol-whip made it unlikely she would try that again. They couldn't take that chance, though; they would move her tonight. One of the men—paunchy, unkempt, with mermaid tattoos all over his body—turned to the other two. "I thought this was gonna be done by now. We were only supposed to have to watch her for a week, Larson told us. And he didn't say nothin' about no search party. Or that she would be such a tough little bitch. She isn't afraid of us. And she's seen our faces. How are we going to stop her from turning us in?"

One of the other two said, "I'm itching to get back on the road. A storage shed isn't my idea of a fun time. I don't know about you guys, but I don't want to sit here much longer. And I don't get my kicks picking on a teenybopper."

The third man, the heaviest set and most slovenly of the three, said, "Well, at least the pay is good. It would take us a month to make as much driving truck as we have from this little gig. And don't worry—by the time I finish threatening that little snot-nosed girl in the other room, she'll be too scared to tell anyone about us."

Lindsey lay on the floor, whimpering. Bones in her face felt broken. It made her hate them even more.

She had completely lost any sense of what day or what time of day it was. She could hear noises that helped a bit. The crows started early. She could hear one particularly noisy crow. They had crows at their home. She thought about how one crow would go from yard to yard finding bird feeders and call to the others when it was successful. Suddenly, she realized that meant she was near a lake. Maybe not her lake, but a lake. Every lake here had people around it. Not all was lost.

The guy who had hit her across the face with his gun, the one she mentally called Moe, entered the room where she was being kept. He took out his cell phone to take a picture.

"Well, little honey. Here we are. Smile for your daddy." When she didn't respond, he kicked her foot. "I said smile for your daddy."

"He's not my dad," she responded defiantly.

"That's okay. He'll know it's you. Unless you don't cooperate and I have to hurt you again. Look up here. I want your daddy to see how beautiful his little girl looks."

22

Hal had been released from jail three days earlier because of a lack of evidence to detain him. He was warned not to leave the county. Today, at his cabin, he stood holding an envelope in his hand. It had been attached to the handle of his screen door when he opened it to get the paper that morning. He knew they were close by, and he was terrified of what was in it. He didn't tell his wife about it. Not wanting to alarm her, he told her he was going to the hardware store. He got in the car and drove a few miles away to a roadside rest stop. Looking at the photo of Lindsey's face, he became sick to his stomach. He stopped the car and got out, vomiting. He could never let his wife see this. And he would have to do what they wanted, or they were all in danger, especially his stepdaughter.

Because Hal worked in a chemistry lab, he had access to chemicals other people didn't. He had supplied these men with lithium in the past. He was able to obtain it through the university in large quantities because it was a research institution. Anyone else ordering it would have raised suspicion. He had to stop getting it because the department chair was beginning to question why Hal was using so much and what he was researching. However, when he told the men he couldn't get the crucial mineral for them, they had abducted his stepdaughter. He had told them he would figure out another way to get what they wanted. They felt he was moving too slowly and decided his stepdaughter was good insurance that he would follow through.

He called the number he had been given, and a gruff man answered.

"It's me."

"Good," the man grunted.

"I need to know that my stepdaughter is still alive."

"She is," the man answered.

"I want her released. I will do what you've asked. Just let her go."

"It's not that easy, Hal. Deliver the goods and we'll let her go. Don't deliver them and you'll find out just how nasty we can be—2:00 tomorrow." The man hung up.

The shipment was arriving this afternoon. The challenge was to make sure it wasn't intercepted. Especially by Carley. He hadn't foreseen her return to the lake. Damn, it was an inconvenient time. He would figure it out. He stopped back at his cabin to let his wife know he was going to check and see how the search was going. Instead, he headed to Fargo, driving carefully, doubling back through country roads. There was no sign of anyone following him. He kept on driving, knowing that, if he were caught, he would immediately be back in jail for breaking the conditions of his release.

Meanwhile, the FBI agent watched the pattern Hal was driving on his screen. The tracking device they had attached was working. He chuckled out loud. Clearly, Hal anticipated being followed. He just didn't anticipate it would be electronically.

The agent loaded the laptop into the front passenger seat so he could follow Hal on the screen and quickly set out. He would arrive at the lab shortly after Hal, but that wasn't all bad. He alerted an agent in the nearby city who would have a detail meet him there. The agent could smell it. Something was going down, and Hal knew what it was. He didn't really believe that Hal was responsible for his stepdaughter's disappearance. He did, however, believe he was at the center of what was happening. Clearly, Hal was a pawn in the drama that was unfolding.

When Hal arrived at the lab, he was dripping with sweat. It wasn't that hot a day outside, but his nerves were getting to him. He looked around carefully for unfamiliar cars, then nonchalantly walked into the building that housed his lab. He was dismayed to be met by his department chair, who led him into an office with two official-looking men.

"Hal, we have to talk," said the department chair.

Two hours later, Hal emerged alone from the lab. Half an hour later, the two FBI agents departed as well.

23

Carley awoke with a start. She didn't know why—she must have had a bad dream. Abigail perked up beside her. She lay back down, trying to think about what she was going to do that day. She remembered—this was the day she was going to help with the search. She looked at her clock. It was only 6:00 a.m.; the search was starting at 8:00. Turning off her alarm, she got up to take a shower.

By 7:00, she was ready to go. She made two sandwiches, packed up a cooler, fed the bird, and picked up Abigail's leash. She figured a dog wouldn't be in the way and might help. Spraying tick spray over her clothes and body, she shuddered at the thought of ticks, knowing there would be a lot of them in the woods where they'd be walking. Then she drove over to pick up Mark at the cabin where he was staying.

When they arrived at the search headquarters, she was pleasantly surprised to see about two hundred people there, ready to help. The search was well organized, with the search area divided up by lakes and by beaches within each lake. People were asked to search the wooded areas behind lake homes and the nearby farmlands. The farmers in the area had agreed to allow their land to be searched, as long as it didn't disrupt their crops. A helicopter crew donated by one of the local TV stations would search the corn rows. By the end of the day, they expected a fifty-mile radius to be thoroughly searched. If they found a shed they couldn't get into or a building that looked suspicious, they were to call the number on the information sheet. They were instructed to find a walking stick and use it to probe any significant piles of leaves. Her heart sank. *Of course, they're searching for a body*, she thought. She shuddered at the image. She held out hope that Lindsey had run away or would be found. What Hal must be going through she could only imagine.

Carley and Mark took the farmland behind their beach as the place they would search, splitting up so they could cover more territory. Using walking sticks distributed by the search organizers, they poked piles of leaves. About three hours later, they came back to their prearranged meeting spot near the farmer's trucking business. She had left the cooler there with sandwiches, dog treats, two beers, and three bottles of water. Mark accepted the water with gratitude. It was a hot, dusty day, and ticks and flies were in abundance. They found a shade tree to eat under. It was Carley's turn to ask him a few questions. What company did he work for, and how did they get involved with the condominiums in the first place? Why were they so certain they would sell? What kind of a market study had they done? What was the DNR's position? What kind of legal battle did he have ahead?

Finally, he raised his hands and said, "I give! Can't we talk about something besides my work and stress?"

She changed the subject to favorite lake sports. Mark didn't strike her as much of a lake person. He didn't strike her as an attorney, either. While he seemed analytical, he didn't have the laser-sharp argumentative approach she was used to with her attorney friends. He was inquisitive and a good listener, but there was something a bit secretive about him that she couldn't quite pinpoint.

After their rest, they continued through the fields. Together, they looked at the trucker's property. It was loaded with buildings, all of them locked. They called the number on the information sheet to report the buildings. Carley decided to try each door and shout out Lindsey's name, just in case she could get an answer.

There was no response from any of the units. She told Mark about hearing some mewing coming from the direction of one of the storage units the day Abigail Rose was lost. He said he found it odd that a kitten would be in a storage unit unless it happened to go in while someone was loading or unloading things from the unit. She agreed. She said she only heard the sound once, so she may have misjudged the direction it was coming from.

By 5:00 p.m., they were both tired but had covered the area they were assigned. They rejoined the search party. There was a barbecue with brats, hot dogs, hamburgers, and beer to thank the people who had completed the search. Also, people were encouraged to report anything unusual. One team found a women's top, but it wasn't the size Lindsey wore. Another team found one lone shoe on the back road. It was a men's shoe, size 11, not likely related to the girl in captivity. All in all, it was a fruitless search, except that everyone could be sure she wasn't being hidden in plain view. There was debate about next steps as many volunteers offered to widen the range of the search. They went home tired that evening. Mark insisted she drive straight back to her lake home, and walked her to the door and waited while she unlocked it. Giving her a quick peck on her cheek, he said, "See you next week," and left. Carley was too tired to give it another thought. Any other time, she might have wondered what the kiss meant. Instead, she slipped into bed, every bone in her body aching, and immediately fell into a deep sleep.

24

The next day, Carley decided to look up the company where Mark worked. She'd be willing to lead a protest against the condominiums, but she was fairly certain she'd missed her chance. The deal was cut last year, when she had been way too busy to even notice what was going on.

She typed in the name of the company. It was based in Chicago and handled major commercial construction litigation as well as running interference on large construction projects. "Owners' rep" was another name for the work they did. They had a combination of legal staff and construction management. Interesting firm. Clearly, they expected this would be a highly controversial project requiring a significant investment to ensure no roadblocks were set up for the construction.

She searched for *Mark Dolan*, but his name didn't come up. *Odd*, she thought. If he were one of the front people for their work, she would expect to find him on the company website. Out of curiosity, she called the corporate headquarters' main number. The operator indicated they didn't have an employee by that name. When she hung up, she took a big gulp. What intuition made her even call and ask? If he didn't work for this company, who was he? And what was his reason for being here now? Did he have a connection with the events that were going on? It made her shudder. She decided she'd better not let on that she knew he didn't work there. She'd better be careful too. He seemed like a nice enough person, but she had misjudged character before.

Carley decided to avoid Mark. When she went out for a run that afternoon, she went the opposite direction of his rented cabin. Likewise, for the next couple of days, she and Abigail avoided any contact with him. It wasn't hard to do.

Things were going exceptionally well for Carley with her work. The VP was ecstatic with the marketing plan. He told her he had another project that might materialize when this one was over. She appreciated hearing that, because she really hadn't begun serious job hunting yet. Perhaps working as a strategic marketing consultant was possible. She'd see what happened in a couple of months but decided she shouldn't stop her job search based on that sole comment.

* * *

Carley felt like she was beginning to settle in. Her garage now remained closed with no intruders. Gordon would be back soon, and she looked forward to seeing what might develop with him. She was starting to meet people through church and on the beach. Most of them were married couples, but they included her in events they were hosting. She saw Jeff, the Realtor, at church one day, but they had just chatted briefly. Mac hadn't been back in touch. That was both a relief and a sadness. She was swimming a mile a day and feeling really in good shape. Trish was coming up soon, and she was getting a lot done. Her budding relationship with Gordon held some promise. Her life wasn't quite the tippy canoe it had been when she first arrived.

She decided to go for a walk, all by herself this time. Abigail had stepped on something sharp and, uncharacteristically, wasn't in the mood for a walk. She limped over to the door, then lay down on the rug in front of it.

"Tomorrow, girl," Carley cooed.

As she walked down the path to the road, Carley was startled by a delivery truck that stopped before she got to the end of the driveway. A young man jumped out, looked at her, and asked if she could accept a package for Arthur Norgren. Carley flushed and then responded, "Why yes. Of course."

"Thanks," he said. "You saved me a trip to the garage."

"The what?" she asked absent-mindedly.

"The garage," the young man responded. "Where I usually leave the packages." He handed her the box and jumped back into his truck.

Carley stood frozen in place. Why would someone send her father a package? He had been dead for two years. She ripped the brown wrapping off the box and read, *Lithium*. Puzzled, she set the package just inside the garage and went back to her run while she contemplated what had just happened.

Partway down the road, Mark Dolan pulled up next to her in his sand-colored sedan. "Hey there," he said. "I'm headed into town to pick up some tools. I hear there's a new ice cream shop. Want to come along?"

She started to say no, then reconsidered. It would give her a chance to ask him some questions. And she certainly was curious. She had no idea who he was or what he was up to. She used to trust her judgment about people. That had all changed.

"Sure," she said, hesitating slightly. She didn't want to give him reason to doubt her. With that, she hopped into his car, and off they drove to Pelican Rapids.

In the car, Carley was glad she didn't have to look Mark in the eye. Somehow, the conversation seemed more casual with a windshield in front of them.

"How are things going with your job?" Carley asked unceremoniously.

"They're fine. Things will start ramping up once the blueprints are on display at the bait shop. People up here are not happy about the project," he said, stating the obvious.

"They're not. And I'm among them. I'm sure you can understand how losing that pristine bay will affect the lake. It's the last undeveloped spot there is. Everything else is built up with homes on small lots. Now it will be overrun by more people."

"Getting to know Pelican Lake a little better, I can see what you mean, but the lake association should have made moves to have that land declared protected. They didn't, and when it went on the market, well, someone was going to buy it."

"I know. No one understood that could happen, especially with high-density housing like condos. I'm not even sure I could work for a company like yours. How do you do it?" Carley pressed.

"Oh, it's not so bad. People get over their discontent once the project is done and there's nothing more to be said about it."

"How do you feel about being associated with something so unpopular? Or isn't it hard, since you don't live here?"

Glancing over at her, Mark commented, "It can be brutal, is that what you mean? Well, it's true that I don't have to live with the outcome, but it will be better than it seems right now. The builder is a good one, and he's concerned about protecting the environment as much as he can."

Carley remained unconvinced. "What will you do when this project is over? Will you go back to Chicago?"

"I'll go wherever the company needs me to go," he remarked. "I wish I could stay. I like the area. But that's not likely. We're not doing many projects up here."

So, he is still working with the company, Carley noted. *Why is the company keeping him hidden?*

Later that day, Carley went over to Jana and Dan's house. "What do you know about Mark?" she asked.

"I don't know," Jana said. "He seems nice enough. He's older than you are, but he's good looking. I've seen him at a couple of barbecues and the beach meeting, and he seems to have made friends with some people around here. Why? You interested?"

She blushed. "No, not in the least. Just wondering."

Carley was quite certain people on the beach were concerned about her being alone. The few people she was close to knew that it was over between her and Mac. The others really didn't know much about her life but always asked in a solicitous way how she was doing and how she managed the cabin alone. She laughed. Of course, she'd learned that she could solve any problem if she was willing to throw enough money at it. This summer, however, money was tight, so she mowed the grass, blew off the deck, weeded the garden, and emptied the gutters by herself. She planned some additional home repair projects, like painting the garage, which was looking very disheveled. The larger cabin would have to wait until next year. It wasn't that bad, but she was much more aware of all that needed to be done since she was here all the time. Home repair was a good break from her marketing work, which required intense concentration. Also, it got her out of her head, which was always a good thing. There was no doubt, however, that she was lonesome. It was hard to be on her own, without anyone really paying attention to whether she was coming or going.

25

By nightfall, Carley was feeling antsy. She really hadn't had contact with much of anyone for several days, except for her brief conversations with her neighbors and with Mark. She called Trish. "When *are* you coming?" she asked pleadingly.

"This weekend, I promise. I have things I have to get done for the wedding in the next few days."

Trish was marrying someone she met through an online dating site. Carley didn't really care for him. She thought he underestimated Trish and overestimated himself, but she wasn't the one who would have to live with him. Her job was to support her good friend.

Carley tossed and turned while she lay in bed. Usually she didn't stew this much, but she was in such an odd place in her life. Contemplating where she should focus her job search, she realized that, with nothing tying her down except a dog and a bird, she could live anywhere. That, in itself, was overwhelming. She still wanted to explore marketing jobs in Fargo. At least she would be near the lake. And Gordon. It was too soon to know if their relationship had promise. It seemed to, but she didn't want to make the same mistake she'd made with Mac. She had committed to him before he had fully committed to her. Her marketing contract ran through the end of the calendar year. Once the lake season ended, she could rent an apartment in Fargo. It was time to get her résumé together and start making contacts that could be helpful.

She found herself thinking about Gordon a lot, but he was at the conference, and it would be a few more days until they talked. They had texted the day he was traveling, but they hadn't connected since then. She hardly knew him, but she knew the attraction she felt for him was strong. She found herself picking up her phone to see if she had missed a call.

Glancing at the clock radio, it was 2:00 a.m. She hadn't had this much trouble sleeping since she'd left Minneapolis. She sighed and punched her pillow. Nothing was that distressing. She was just in a transition. She had to believe everything would work out.

In the not-so-far-off distance, she could hear the noise of semitrucks. She hadn't heard that noise in the night before, but that was the problem of having a "truck farm" nearby. Directly outside her window, she heard a rustling noise—most likely a raccoon. Then she heard a sound like water from an erratic sprinkler. *Strange*, she thought. No, it wasn't any of her pipes. The noise came from outside. Was it coming from the outdoor pump? Her neighbor's pump? Suddenly, she heard a *whoosh*. She jumped from her bed as she watched the window explode with light. The garage was on fire. She grabbed her bathrobe and ran to the garage, stopping to grab a fire extinguisher from the closet by the door. The blaze was too big for her extinguisher. When something inside the garage exploded, neighbors began rushing out of their homes.

Mark was one of the first on the scene. "Are you okay?" he asked. Carley noticed he was fully dressed, while everyone else was in bathrobes and pajamas.

Realizing she could smell gasoline, she shrieked. The noise had been the sound of someone sprinkling gas around her garage. She ran back to the house. Was there gas surrounding it too? She raced inside, scooped up Abigail Rose—who looked very nervous—and grabbed Prattle's cage. She wasn't going to let them burn to death.

Racing to Jana and Dan's home, she pleaded, "Here, take them. Please?" They quickly grabbed the animals and brought them inside. She ran back up to the garage.

About twelve people were now standing around. The fire truck came speeding up the road with lights flashing. The firefighters quickly disembarked from their truck and ran the hose connected to a pump into the lake.

"Do you have any idea what caused the fire?" one of the firefighters asked.

"I think it was started by gasoline," she answered.

He yelled to his companions to get the foam solution started first. However, the wood of the garage was burning furiously, and the smoke was billowing up into the crisp night air.

She was stunned. Why would anyone do this?

It took about two hours for the firefighters to get everything under control. They sprayed foam around the house to make sure the fire wouldn't spread. By 5:00 a.m., the fire was still smoldering but well contained. It would take a few more hours before it would completely extinguish. She was in shock. Jana and Dan stayed by her. Mark was off on the side, talking with Ben and some of the other neighbors who were coming and going. No one could believe what had happened. The garage was in shambles. Carley surveyed the ashes of the garage and the remnants of her father's life that were strewn around, sat down on the wet grass, and started to sob. Almost everything was lost. None of it was that important; it was just so many reminders of her past that she was consumed by an overwhelming sense of grief and sadness. And anger. Who did this? And why?

By 7:00 a.m., the firefighters had finished their job. The remains of the garage were barely smoldering. The fire marshal had finished his report. Other neighbors had come by. Those who were there shortly after the garage ignited had already headed back home to go back to bed. Carley felt numb. It was so hard to fathom that anyone would want to set this fire. The sheriff had asked her a few questions and talked with a few people standing around. He seemed satisfied that there was nothing more that he could do right now, told her Carley was sorry for her losses, gave her his card, and asked her to call if she had any additional information.

While the firefighters had said it was safe for her to stay there, she didn't know if she would ever be able to stay there again. Jana and Dan told her she could sleep in their guest bedroom. She was exhausted, and a clean bed sounded wonderful. She accepted their offer, and soon all of them retreated to get some sleep.

26

The next afternoon, things looked only slightly brighter. Carley called her insurance agent, who told her everything would be covered, assuming the investigation revealed she hadn't started the fire herself. While she couldn't save much from the garage, she was able to retrieve several things that meant something to her. None of them were valuable, just highly sentimental. Her mother's cedar chest was miraculously only slightly burned, and everything in it, while smoky, was fine. She salvaged a piece of her father's wool plaid shirt. Plus, the hand tools that had belonged to her paternal grandfather had survived. She started making a list of everything that was ruined. Most of those things were power tools, easily replaced, or miscellaneous parts, paints, boxes to be recycled. She was surprised by how little actual value the garage held. Her father's file cabinets and their contents were destroyed, but she wouldn't understand anything in those files anyway. Most of them were his research records, and Gordon had copies of what the university didn't have. She felt good about that. But the fire was totally discombobulating. Her body still felt in shock.

The sheriff stopped by again later that afternoon. He recommended she have a security camera installed, especially the kind that emitted a buzz when it sensed movement. She could see how that could easily drive her crazy, but said she would do what he suggested. Also, he suggested she install a panic button that tied

MURDER at PELICAN LAKE

directly into the police department. While he hadn't impressed her in the past, she was glad for his attention now.

After the sheriff left, Mark walked over and asked if she'd like to get a bite to eat at the store. She was hungry but couldn't imagine how she'd carry on a conversation with him right now. She was exhausted and leery of just about everyone, especially him. Why had he arrived on the scene so fast, fully dressed, at that time of night?

Plus, she thought about the package she had set inside the door of the garage. Lithium. Was that an explosive? She racked her brain, digging back into what she knew from high school chemistry. She doubted it, given how it was packed. If it were, it would have a warning label or a sticker indicating it was explosive, she figured. Oddly, she hadn't found any traces of it after the fire. Should she be worried? And why was lithium delivered to her father? Was this part of his research? Had someone not been notified of his death? She thought of how hard she had worked to make sure that all her father's accounts and credit cards were canceled. She could hardly hold her head up any longer, much less figure out why her father was receiving a package now.

27

It was 2:00 a.m. when the semi rolled into the truck farmer's storage area. Two men were waiting there to unload the machines. They were relieved to be out of the storage shed, away from monitoring the girl, doing something physical. They quickly opened the doors of the truck and started unloading it.

By 3:30 a.m., they were finished. Step one of the master plan was complete. While they didn't understand all the cloak-and-dagger secrecy, they would do what they were told. Machines instead of drugs. Maybe the head honcho was going legit.

28

The next day, Carley arose determined to get control of what she could. At first, she was terrified by what had happened. Now, she was mad. She was mad someone intentionally burned down her garage. She was mad someone ruined her sense of security at the lake. She was mad she felt so off balance now. She couldn't trust the sheriff to protect her, so she would have to protect herself.

She drove into Fergus Falls and went immediately to a sporting goods store, where she planned to buy a gun. They directed her to another store, since they had only rifles for deer and duck hunting. Carley wanted a small revolver she could keep near her bed or carry in her purse. At the next stop, she found one that fit the bill. The clerk informed her she wouldn't be able to take it with her that day. To buy it, she'd have to get a permit to purchase from the local police department. That would take three to four weeks to process. To carry it, she would need a permit to carry from the county sheriff's department. That required taking a class. Neither was a quick solution. He asked if she knew how to use the gun and suggested she work with an instructor while she was getting the paperwork completed. He cited statistics of how many people were killed by their own weapons. It was startling, and she knew his advice was good. He handed her a list of places she could go to get help. One of them was a place that had an outdoor range on farmland not far from her lake home where they had a selection of guns she could try out. She was certain her father had a gun in the garage, but it hadn't turned up as they were sifting through the rubble. She'd have to get the paperwork going if she wanted to purchase one. It would take a while. For now, she'd settle for trying some guns out.

When she arrived at the range, she was quite startled to see Mark there. He was wearing a headset over his ears and was doing target practice. He was quite good; most of his shots were in the bull's-eye. She wondered why he needed a gun in his line of work. Did most corporate attorneys carry a gun? One of her attorney friends had been threatened by a client whose case he lost. Another had prosecuted a drug dealer and, after he won the case, always carried a gun. Perhaps it wasn't such a far-fetched thing for Mark to want to protect himself.

Mark's surprise was evident when Carley stepped into her shooting lane next to his. The instructor worked with her on how to hold the gun, how to cock it, how to aim it. He demonstrated several shots for her, then helped her aim and had her fire a few shots. The first several missed the target altogether. It was much harder to shoot than she expected. However, she started homing in on the target and eventually the bull's-eye. She'd always had good hand-eye coordination, and it didn't fail her now. She graduated to the moving target and had some success there. The instructor gave her a few pointers, then left to help the next student.

Carley kept practicing until she got the feel of it. Pulling the trigger wasn't so hard—though the gun had a fair amount of recoil—it was the icy feeling she had about the thought of ever having to use it. That someone might be such a threat to her that she would consider using a gun was very unnerving.

Soon she had rhythm to her shots and was even hitting the moving target. There was one more level of expertise at the beginner level, but Carley decided to leave that for another day. She was sure she would improve, but that wasn't what worried her. Could she defend herself if she needed to? Could she really pull the trigger if there was a person in front of her? Could she control her adrenaline enough to even get close? It was much easier to hit a target than it would be to shoot a real person. If she was going to own a gun, she had to be comfortable using it. Carley decided she'd better come back and practice a few more times. The thought of even owning a gun made her uneasy.

Removing his goggles and headset, Mark said to Carley, "Well, I wouldn't want to meet you in a dark alley!"

"Ha! Looks like you're the expert here! What made you take this sport up?" Carley questioned him.

"Oh, I deal with unpopular projects, so I decided a long time ago I'd better be able to defend myself. After what happened at your cabin last night, I came over to brush up on my skills."

"Well, it looks like that worked," Carley remarked.

"Yeah, it came back fast. How about you? Are you sure you want to pack heat?"

She laughed. "I don't want to be caught off guard again. There are too many weird things going on around here lately. Maybe the word will get around that I have a gun." She was glad he would think that, even though she didn't own one yet.

"How about a cup of coffee or a glass of wine?" Mark suggested.

"I can't," she responded. "I really have a lot to do still today. I have a security company coming to my cabin in about forty-five minutes."

"Well, you are taking precautions. I don't blame you. Last night was frightening. The pyromaniac must have been scared off. At least he didn't set fire to your cabin." He shuddered as he thought about what might have happened.

She paled at the thought but didn't indicate she was wondering if he had something to do with the fire. It was best to keep that to herself until she understood what was happening and who was behind it. She couldn't imagine why anyone would want to hurt her or her property. For now, she would stay with Jana and Dan until the security system was installed.

29

It had been a week and a half since Gordon had been in her garage reviewing her father's records. She hoped he was able to get everything he needed because there was no going back. She probably should have offered to ship her father's file cabinet to the university, since their records were disappointingly inaccurate, according to Gordon. Well, it was too late for that now. She wondered if Gordon had even heard about the fire since he had been in Colorado, but she'd expected him to be back by now.

When she called his cell phone, her call went immediately into voice mail. After several hours without a return call, she decided to call him at his office. The phone rang and rang. Apparently, he wasn't in the office. She supposed faculty were lucky that way. They weren't usually accountable for their summers and could take off to do research—or just take off. It was probably just as well he wasn't answering. He had told her he would call when he returned. She didn't want him to think she didn't trust that.

A voice interrupted her chain of thought, saying, "Chemistry department, Dr. Locklear's office."

It was a voice she recognized. "Helen—it's Carley."

"Well, hi there, sweetie! It's been a long time since I've talked with you."

"I didn't expect to get you, Helen. I thought I would get Gordon's voice mail."

"Well, he's gone so much this summer, I had his phone line transferred to me. He asked me if I could stay on top of his calls. What can I help you with?"

"I wanted to let Gordon know what happened to my father's records."

"Okay. Do you want me to give him a message?"

"Sure, that would be great. He came by about two weeks ago to copy some of my father's files, and two days ago, my garage was burned down. Everything was lost. I just wanted to let him know how glad I was he got what he needed. And I wondered if I could get a copy of what he has."

"It couldn't have been Dr. Locklear you're talking about. Are you thinking about Dr. Emerson or Dr. Matthews?"

"No, why?" Carley asked, puzzled.

"Because Dr. Locklear has been in Brussels all summer. He left at the end of May and won't get back until the end of August, just before classes start up."

"What?" Carley asked incredulously. "But I just met him a couple of weeks ago. He came over and told me he needed some of my dad's records because the university files were incomplete."

"No, I think you must have him confused with someone else. I'll ask around and see if someone else put a call in to you."

"Thanks, Helen," Carley said, quickly getting off the phone. Either Gordon was letting Helen believe he was in Brussels for the summer or he wasn't who he said he was. What the hell was going on?

30

"At last! You're here!" Carley cried as she ran out of the cabin to greet the woman getting out of her car.

"I know," Trish said. "But I didn't realize I was coming to the end of the world. Whew—that's quite a drive."

Carley hugged Trish. It was great to have someone staying with her. She was a little nervous about how comfortable Trish would be, given what had transpired as of late. However, Trish was undaunted and had decided, if anything, Carley needed her now more than ever.

"Nice garage," Trish stated dryly as she scanned its charred remains.

They had made great plans for the three-day weekend. First on their schedule was a trip to Vergas to check out a special dress shop and an artisan who produced beautiful glass and copper artwork on a farm outside of town. After that, they would go to Detroit Lakes for the department store's annual shoe sale, then to the farmers' market and back to Pelican. The rest of the day would be spent boating and jet skiing on the very calm lake. It was a beautiful day, and both Trish and Carley were glad for the chance to be together.

As they rode along the country roads, Trish talked giddily about her upcoming wedding plans. At thirty-three, she felt a little sheepish about how excited she was. It would be a destination wedding in Costa Rica for their immediate families and just a few close friends. Carley had agreed to be her maid of honor. Trish already had her dress and had picked out what she wanted for Carley. The color would be fuchsia. Carley marveled to herself that this color looked good on very few people and especially not her. At least it would look appropriate in the tropical climate. She had always wanted to go to Costa Rica on a romantic getaway. Oh well. That could still happen in the distant future. Even in that setting, she doubted that she would like Bill, Trish's fiancé, any more than she did now. She suspected Trish felt about Mac the way she felt about Bill.

"So, tell me about this man you've been seeing," Trish said. "Are you falling for him?"

"He's good looking, but that wasn't really my primary attraction to him. He's very smart, fun, adventurous, spontaneous. He's helped me explore this vicinity, and we've really had a good time together. He drives a jazzy sports car, but it's because of a love he shared with his grandfather. I know what the real hook is for me: my father mentored him, and my father was a very good judge of people. I almost feel as though he's the one who brought us together."

"You, my dear friend, are a hopeless romantic." Trish laughed. "But you never know. Your dad was a very special man, and he cared so much about you. I wouldn't put it past him," she said smilingly.

"There's just one catch. I tried to call him at the university a couple of days ago. I got ahold of Helen, the office manager, who insisted it couldn't possibly be Gordon I had met, since Gordon is in Brussels for the summer. I don't know if Gordon came back and didn't tell her, or if there is something else going on," Carley admitted.

Trish was surprisingly philosophical about it. "Give him a chance to explain. There may be something going on and there may not. Are you sure he's not married?"

That had crossed Carley's mind, but she didn't want to give it too much thought. It wasn't in her to be the other woman; it just wasn't part of her chemistry. But honesty was, and she was really concerned about what was going on. Whom was he leading on? She deeply hoped she wasn't the one.

"And then there's Mac," Trish said tentatively.

"Ha. I heard from him the other day. He called me at 7:00 a.m. because he knew I can hardly see straight that time of the morning, much less say anything biting to him."

"Why did he call?"

"Because he discovered some boxes in a storage closet that we had both forgotten about."

"I think it's more than that. I think he still has a thing for you."

"No, it was about boxes. Period."

"I bumped into him a couple of weeks ago. He seemed glad to see me and couldn't ask me enough questions about you. I think he's not completely over you yet."

"Well, you could have fooled me. I don't know if it matters. I doubt that I could ever trust him again anyway. I just hope he isn't the only serious love I'll ever have."

"You've got to be kidding," Trish countered. "You can do much better."

Trish's reaction startled her. Carley didn't want to talk about Mac anymore, so she said, "Come on. Let's get this weekend going." And with that, they headed to Vergas to shop.

In Vergas, reward posters lined the street poles. The residents had held several fund raisers to secure a significant amount of money for anyone with any information about Lindsey's disappearance. Normally a hub of vacation activity, the town was subdued. Clearly, Lindsey's disappearance had cast a pall over the area. It was sobering, and they left without doing any shopping.

After their outing, Carley and Trish retreated to the cabin for a respite. They floated on water rafts, went for a long cocktail cruise, and spent Saturday night at the pizza/taco hot spot on the lake.

The restaurant, which had a live band and a great bar, was hopping until well past midnight. They had fun meeting new people and dancing, sometimes together. Jeff had been at the restaurant with a group of people. He came over to say hello to Carley, and the two of them danced a couple of songs. She suspected one of the women in the group was watching his every move. As Carley and Trish drove the boat back to the cabin, the moon lit a path along the clear, still water.

The next day was rainy, so they sat around inside, talking, sharing life dreams, playing Scrabble. When Trish left, Carley felt as if she were the cheese standing alone. Unexpected pangs of lonesomeness overcame her. Maybe she needed to spend a little time back in Minneapolis. She hadn't shared her concerns about Bill with Trish. She had done that once, and it nearly cost her their friendship. *Hopefully, everything will work out between them,* she thought. If not, she would just have to be there for her. What if Mac wanted to get back together? Could she ever find her way back to him? She doubted it, but time could really change things, she knew.

31

The weekend had gone so quickly while Trish was there that Carley didn't have time to swim across the lake as she had hoped. It would have to wait until Trish's next trip up. Plus, the weather had become very windy and had suddenly turned cold, even for late June. Not great swimming weather.

It was only midmorning, and Carley couldn't figure out what to do with herself. It was a gloomy, gray day, with no activity on the lake except for one fishing boat near the middle, and she knew she wouldn't be able to concentrate on her work. Abigail looked at her expectantly, but Carley indicated they weren't going for a walk. The dog traipsed over to her bed and lay down dejectedly.

Carley had found it disturbing that, as far as she knew, there was no activity by the police to find out what was dropped off the boat the night she saw it. *Geez*, she thought. Small-town police must not approach things the same way they would in a larger city. She knew her friend Matt, who was a police officer in St. Paul, would have been all over it if he had been at the other end of that call.

She was curious. Admittedly, it was most likely nothing. Her conclusion that it was construction materials being dropped overboard seemed the most plausible explanation. She was convinced everyone dropped something off a boat into the lake at some time. The lake was so clear now because of the zebra mussels that she wondered if she might see even shadows at that depth. She estimated they must have been in about twenty-five feet of water. Digging into the storage closet, she came up with a relief map of the lake showing different depths and where there were drop-offs where walleye might be hiding. Her guess was a good one. It looked like it would be about twenty-five feet deep.

She had a high-powered depth finder on the fishing boat that had belonged to her dad. Enlisting Abigail as part of her cover, she took the dog and her fishing pole down to the boat. Lazily trolling down the lake and making it appear as if she were fishing would hopefully not draw attention to what she was doing. Not having used a depth finder before, she wished she knew where the instruction manual was. Probably, it burned with the garage.

At last, she was off. She overshot the place where she was quite sure the bag had been dropped off the boat. It was in a depth of water where muskie hung out, so she smugly decided fishing was a good ruse. Unfortunately, the depth finder showed a lot of variation on the lake floor. She had hoped it would be more obvious. There were many blips that represented fish, though it was hard to tell their size. After she had made three passes over the spot, she decided to make just one more since she didn't want to draw attention to what she was doing.

Finally, she was rewarded. An odd blip appeared on the floor of the lake. It appeared to be six or seven feet long. She couldn't quite tell, but it was enough to pique her interest. She registered the coordinates on the GPS so she could find it another day and proceeded to troll back to her home. Whatever they had dropped off the pontoon was still there, undisturbed by the police, just as she suspected. She hoped she hadn't raised any suspicions.

At home, the project consumed her thoughts. Having traveled to the Virgin Islands several times with Mac, she owned her own scuba equipment. While she was experienced at diving, she didn't feel comfortable diving into the water in the dead of night. She decided she'd go diving early in the morning when the fewest people were up and around. She still had one full canister of oxygen. Since the sun rose around 5:30, she could be out on the lake by 5:00 before anyone was up and be ready to jump in the lake at the first sign of sunlight. After testing the equipment, she packed up the boat for her early-morning adventure.

What seemed like a good idea at night wasn't quite as exciting the next morning. The wind was from the north, and it was already blowing about fifteen miles per hour. That was enough to create waves that could develop into whitecaps. By 4:45 a.m., she was fully loaded into her fishing boat, dressed in a dark wet suit, and pushed away from the dock. As she made her way over the spot, she cut the engine and dropped the anchor. Adjusting the fish finder, she checked to make sure she was at the right coordinates. She was. She put the diving flag and its float on the opposite side of the boat from the shore so it wouldn't be obvious to a casual observer. She then anchored two ropes to the boat. As the sun sliced over the horizon, she donned her goggles and flippers and gently slipped into the water.

Following the anchor rope down, she was disappointed by how dark and hazy the water was. Her underwater flashlight helped a bit, but it wasn't as easy to see the lake bottom as she had hoped. Weeds were growing up three or four feet off the bottom. She swam about five feet farther out from the boat. At last, she had success. It looked like a body bag, dark and lumpy, nestled among the weeds. Her heart felt like it was going to explode out of her wet suit. What if it was Lindsey? How could she ever live with this moment? Maybe she should have insisted the police come with her, but it was a little late for those thoughts now. Plus, the police, for whatever reason, hadn't shown an interest in what was dropped. At least, not yet.

She quickly went back to the surface of the water to figure out what she was going to do. Grabbing the side of the boat, she reached into the back for the two ropes. Using her knowledge of sailor knots she'd learned years earlier, she quickly created two nooses she could wrap around each end of the bag in the water. The trick would be stabilizing the bag enough to secure the ropes. It took a couple of attempts, but she managed to loop a rope around each end of the bag. Getting back into the boat was a bit of a challenge, and she scraped her shin as she pushed herself over the gunnel. Quickly she pulled at the ropes until the package surfaced. She was right. It was indeed a very heavy, lumpy body bag.

32

Her heart was pounding so hard it felt like a small drum banging in her ears. She hadn't fully thought through what she would do if she found something. Not wanting to bring the body bag into the boat, she was concerned someone would spot her recent discovery. She was conspicuous enough given her scuba attire. She hoped she had gone unseen; after all, it was barely sunrise, but she was quite sure someone would notice if she tried to drag the bag up on her dock. Pulling on the two ropes, she secured the bag close to the boat, just below the water's surface. She would slowly drive the boat to the landing at the end of the beach and hide the bag in the overgrown brush until she could come back and retrieve it.

When she approached the beach landing, she jumped out of the boat and steered it toward the shore. No one else was in the vicinity. Grabbing two life preservers from the bottom of the boat, she maneuvered one at each end of the bag and floated it the rest of the way into shore. As she lifted the bag, all the air escaped from her body like a balloon with a fast leak. It wasn't a body at all. The bag, which had all the appearances of a body bag, had metal inside. She was surprised by the disappointment that flooded over her. She had been terrified that it was a body, and now that it wasn't, she felt let down. Assuming she had just cracked the case of what happened to Lindsey, Carley was equally relieved it wasn't her. Perhaps Lindsey was still alive. And yet Carley was a little

sorry it wasn't something more exciting than the construction materials she had originally suspected.

Still, she steered the bag among the trees growing over the
water and pulled it up on shore, hidden from view. Jumping back
into her boat, she headed to her dock about half a bay away.

Once there, she put the boat on the boat lift, removed her
wet suit, and got her car keys. When she returned to the landing,
she awkwardly pulled the bag into the back of her trunk. It was
cumbersome and very heavy, full of metal and water. She slightly
opened the zipper to let the water cascade out, making it easier
to maneuver. *It must weigh over a hundred pounds*, she thought as
she struggled to get it into the trunk. Finally, with a big clunk, she
managed to lob the package over the rim of the trunk. She drove
back home with her treasure so she could figure out what else to do.

In her driveway, she couldn't resist taking a look at what she
had uncovered. Unzipping the bag in the trunk, she was puzzled
by what she found. It wasn't really like anything she had seen before. Suddenly, a voice said, "So, what are you carting around in
that trunk of yours?"

She felt like Mark had purposefully snuck up quietly near her
car so he could see what she had in the trunk.

"Oh, not much," she said breezily.

"Anything you need help with?" he queried as he moved closer
to her trunk.

"Nope," she said as she slammed the trunk shut. "I was just
getting some things ready to take to Goodwill."

"Oh, I've got a few things I've been meaning to get rid of. Let
me know when you're going, and I'll come along."

"Sure thing," she replied, though she knew she would do
nothing of the sort.

After a while, when she was certain Mark wasn't in the immediate area, Carley went for a drive. Taking back roads, she drove
until she came to a roadside rest area. She wanted to be somewhere
safe, out in the open but away from traffic. She pushed the release

button for her trunk, popping the lid open. Surveying the area to make sure she hadn't been followed, she began to explore the black bag and what was in it. The first piece of metal she pulled out was very deformed. It looked like it had been in an explosion. The second piece looked part of a metal box with a lid that had also been blown apart. The metal was covered with a charred substance and had several very sharp, jagged edges as if something had torn right through it. In all, there were about eight pieces with similar markings, all about three feet long and six to eight inches wide. Suddenly, a chill went up and down her spine. She had seen one of these before—in the ruins of her garage after the big fire. There it was again—the garage. But why would someone want to conceal this metal? What in the world was it from? Certainly, an explosion. But what was so important about the metal that it had to be hidden in the lake? Why hadn't they just taken it to the local dump?

She drove around lake country for about an hour, pondering what she should do. She didn't really know what she had here. Should she bring it to the sheriff? Her instincts said otherwise. Her other encounters with him had been unsettling. Where else could she turn?

That night, she lay awake for quite a while. So much had happened in a short period of time. She had gotten the cabin up and running; the garage, which seemed to be the center of some attention, was burned to the ground; and she thought she was falling in love. *Thought.* Past tense. What was it with these men and their alter egos? Mac certainly had one, Gordon wasn't being honest with either her or the department, and Mark didn't work for the company he said he did. Wasn't anyone trustworthy anymore?

Suddenly, she heard Prattle flapping in her cage. Keeping the lights off, Carley grabbed her cell phone and moved warily downstairs toward the kitchen. The moon was hidden behind clouds and, through the windows, the yard was dark. She didn't bother to draw the curtains at night. Abigail came trotting behind her to see what was going on, oblivious to any threat of danger. Carley whispered to her to come, and she did. Suddenly, Abigail looked sharply toward the side door and started to growl, then emitted a couple of sharp barks.

Quickly, Carley dialed 911, grabbed Abigail, went back up into her bedroom, and locked the door. She wished she had been able to buy a gun. She wasn't sure she could use one, but she wished she at least had that choice. Now was the moment she needed it. The new security system was on, but what good would that do to stop someone from breaking in? When 911 answered, she gave them her address, which was a fire number. Twelve minutes later, the sheriff was at her door. If there had been an intruder, a lot could have happened in twelve minutes, Carley thought dryly.

"What's going on? I understand you think someone was trying to break in," the sheriff remarked. "Tell me what happened exactly."

"I was in the house alone, and my bird started to flap her wings."

"Well, she is a bird, after all," the sheriff commented with a deadpan expression.

"Yes, of course, but if you've ever been around animals, you get to know their habits. This bird is completely quiet at night. I think it's to prevent predators from knowing she's here. Anyway, Prattle started to flap her wings. When I came downstairs, I didn't see anything because it was so dark out. I whispered to my dog, and she came over to me. Then suddenly she turned and started growling at the side door. She never does that unless something scares her. I heard a noise like someone bumping the door handle. I can't be sure," Carley said nervously.

The sheriff took out his spotlight and walked around the house, checking all the shrubs and around the neighbors' homes.

"I think it's a critter. We have a lot of raccoons out here. Sometimes they even try to open doors. I wouldn't worry about it if I were you. I know you're probably nervous after what happened to your garage, but I don't see anything amiss around here. Call me if you hear anything else. Just keep your outdoor lights on."

She lay awake for the rest of the night, trying to comprehend what was going on. Something terrible was happening around her. She didn't think she should stay here anymore. She vowed to call Matt, the police officer in St. Paul, to get his advice. A girl was missing, her garage had burned down, and she was quite sure someone was trying to break in to her lake home. Coincidences? Maybe. But what could the connections possibly be? Why so much interest in the garage? Why were the men around her so mysterious? What did any of this have to do with her? Suddenly, a plan came to her. By then, it was dawn, and Carley fell into a fitful sleep.

33

She awoke around 10:00 a.m., exhausted from the events of the previous night. Immediately, she picked up her cell phone and called Matt. She and Matt had grown up together in Fargo, and both later ended up in the Twin Cities for their jobs. After attending the police academy, he joined the St. Paul police force at the age of twenty-two. Currently, he was dating a woman Carley had helped him meet. He was someone she would trust with her life. When they connected, she explained what had happened at the lake and how worried she was. Matt was quiet, then told her he thought she should get out of there. Carley explained she didn't really have anyplace else to go and didn't really want to leave. With a sigh of affectionate frustration, Matt said he would do a little checking and get back to her as soon as he could.

About an hour later, her phone rang. It was Matt. "Well, I have some interesting news. I don't know what all is going on in your area, but the FBI is involved. That doesn't seem too unusual, given that there's a kidnapping of a young girl, but it's more than that. No one up there would talk. I know someone in the FBI, and he's being very closemouthed. I suggest you drive into Fargo and meet with the FBI to see if they can shed any light on it for you. They may be happy to talk with you since you've had a couple of incidents there. Funny thing—there was no incident report that the sheriff came out to visit you last night."

"Well, maybe he hasn't had time to do the paperwork yet," she suggested.

"That's not how it works. He might want to take time to fill out more complete paperwork, but there would always be an immediate report filed. There was nothing. Nada."

With that, Carley swallowed hard, thanked Matt, hung up, and got dressed. She started to put on jeans, then decided she may need to look more credible than that. She chose slacks, a tank top, and a jacket. She put out extra food for both pets in case she came back late.

As Carley drove into Fargo, she called Helen on her way. "Is there any chance I could meet with Dean Anderson anytime today? It's urgent."

"Just a minute. I'll check, sweetie," Helen murmured. A few minutes elapsed. "He has a short break in his schedule around 11:30 this morning. Would that work?"

Carley jumped at the chance to see him. "Absolutely. I'll see you at 11:30, Helen. Thank you. I appreciate your help."

It took about forty-five minutes to drive into Fargo. It was now 10:30. She stopped into a coffee shop to use their Wi-Fi. With a sense of determination, she found the address and phone of the regional FBI office and called the receptionist, who said she would have someone get back to her.

By 11:15, Carley had her ducks in a row and drove to the university to meet with the dean. He was very happy to see her. He'd known Carley since she was a baby; he and her father had been very close friends. After getting caught up on recent events in each other's lives, Carley said, "It's great to see you, Dean Anderson, but this isn't really a social call. Some very strange things have been going on at my lake home. Some of them involve my father, though I don't know how or why." She filled him in on some of the highlights. "You know I'm not a scientist. I have an idea of some of the things he was working on, but can you give me an overview of his research?"

Dean Anderson took a long breath. "Well, let me give you the condensed version of what he was doing. Your father had ties to the Department of Defense and a significant government research contract. He had been working on ways to both locate and neutralize IED's, improvised explosive devices, like pipe bombs. Three of his patents were for a new handheld spectrometer, a device that can identify the atomic composition of liquids. This is important to the Department of Defense, so they can detect the presence of highly explosive liquids. Spectrometers have been around for a long time, but your dad was trying—with some success, I might add—to develop a model that was mobile and highly usable. The applications were potentially huge; the Department of Transportation could use it at truck stops, for instance, to scan their loads for dangerous liquids. It was very cutting-edge work. The Department of Defense felt his research held great promise for identifying some of the most easily accessible types of homemade bombs. It had uses with other chemicals as well; I won't go into all the applications, but you can see it had great potential. Tell me, what is your concern?"

"My father had a file cabinet with his research records stored at the lake. That file cabinet was burned in a garage fire. I'm concerned you won't have all the official records of his work."

"I didn't know about that. We have a copy of all his research here. Your father was very thorough. When I talked to him several years ago, he understood the importance of confidentiality. He must have thought the lake would be a safe place to store what he was working on. He was no dummy."

"Tell me about Gordon Locklear. Is he in town? Has he been to the university this summer?"

"Why Gordon? What do you need to know about him?"

"He's been at my lake home, looking over my father's records. We spent a fair amount of time together. Helen told me he's been in Brussels."

"It's very odd that he would go to your cabin to see records when we have all your father's relevant documents here. He never told me about wanting to do that. Yes, he has been in Brussels. I don't know exactly how long he's been gone. He may have come home for a few days to break up his trip. Why don't you call his wife, Jane, and find out more from her? Helen will have their home phone number."

With that information, Carley blanched. So, it was true; he was a player. Her stomach rose up into her throat. She was not going to cry. Why had she let him get close to her so fast? It was hard to focus now, but she had a lot more to ask.

"What about the device? Who's working on that now? And what about the patents?"

Dean Anderson looked a little uneasy. "Well, we're considering that right now. Of course, the university wants to continue his good work."

"Who would do that work?" she asked.

"That's what we're considering right now. It made sense that it would be Hal, but he's not nearly the scientist your father was."

"Why not Gordon?"

"Well," Dean Anderson responded, "it just wouldn't make sense given that his research interests are so different from your father's. His work is around biodegradable products in the production of plastic, not in spectrometry, like your father's and Hal's."

Carley's head was spinning. So why had Gordon spent two weeks poring over her father's records? It just didn't make any sense.

The idea of Hal continuing her father's work also gave her pause. She knew her father's patents could be potentially valuable. The estate attorney had talked with her and her brother about them because they were named in her father's will. Without a plan to manufacture his patented projects, he felt it would take considerably more resources than they had to realize any gain from them. Patents weren't really this attorney's area of expertise, nor was it theirs. Her brother, John, an English professor, had little interest in pursuing them. On the other hand, it sounded like the university might be exploring their rights with his patents. She wished she knew a good patent attorney now.

"I'm going over to talk with the FBI this afternoon. Is there anything else I should know?" Carley asked.

"I'll have to think about it. I'm sure there's more. I'm sorry for all you've been going through. I'll let you know after I've had time to think about it."

On her way out of the office, Carley stopped by Helen's desk and asked for Gordon's home phone number. She wasn't sure what she would do with it, but she felt better having it in her possession. As she left the university, she felt step one was complete, but the visit had created more questions than answers. The dean seemed genuinely surprised to learn of the existence of her dad's records. She liked and trusted the dean and was glad they'd had the chance to talk. She was confident he would get in touch with her if there was something she should know. She had learned that Gordon had a wife, that he was supposed to be in Brussels, and he didn't have clearance from the university to photocopy her father's materials. Her father's research wasn't even related to his. Perhaps Gordon was trying to advance his career without the dean's support. No matter what, he had proven to be a schmuck, a conniver, and an adulterer. She might have to swear off all men. Should she call him? Text him? Maybe block him. Plus, she now had a sense of urgency about finding an attorney to represent herself and her brother.

She pulled into the parking lot of the FBI office, a very nondescript office in a bank building. Nothing about it indicated it was FBI except the very official seal on the door.

Carley entered the office and told the receptionist she had called for an appointment but hadn't heard back from anyone. Whom could she talk with about the events happening in Otter Tail County?

The receptionist asked her to wait just a minute. She called someone on the phone and told the person she was there. Carley flipped through a *National Geographic* on the coffee table in front of her. Suddenly, the door opened, and out came an agent to greet her.

The agent was Mark Dolan.

34

Carley was stunned. "This explains a little of my confusion. No wonder you weren't on the payroll of the company you said you worked for."

"You checked me out?" Mark asked with a sly smile.

Carley, uncharacteristically at a loss for words, ignored his smile and demanded, "So, what are you up to? And should I be worried?"

Mark motioned to her to sit down, and he took a seat near her. "We have an investigation going on. It's been going on for a while. I'm really not at liberty to tell you the whole story."

"Well, I came here to talk with you—someone—about what has been happening, and I have some information that you might not know about. But I must confess, I'm having a hard time getting over the fact that it's you here. Honestly, I thought *you* were into something shady! So, tell me something that makes me believe you're going to help, or I'll take my information somewhere else."

"I'll give you a couple of highlights; I just can't share all of it with you. I started out following a drug case, drugs that were being sent from Minneapolis to the oil fields of North Dakota. We had suspicions that a couple of people on your beach were involved. Drugs were being smuggled in other shipments being carried by semis to the oil fields. But now the case has taken a turn. I don't know what to make of it yet. Your return here caused a stir," Mark continued. "When you first arrived, I wasn't sure why you were back, and I had to be careful. You became close to the main person I've been following. Unusual deliveries were coming to your garage. It was an odd coincidence, but I didn't know how you were involved. Once it was apparent you really had decided just to live here for the summer and weren't connected with what was happening, keeping you safe became a priority."

"Well, great job with the garage fire. Weren't you at all concerned that I could have been hurt or even killed?" Carley asked incredulously.

"We have surveillance cameras on the beach. One is pointed at the entrance of your garage and picks up activity down the street. We monitor them twenty-four hours a day."

Carley felt anger swelling up in her throat. "Really? And you didn't think I had a right to know what has happening?"

"We had to be sure you weren't involved. There are a lot of moving parts to this puzzle, and many high-profile people are involved."

"Really? Like who?"

"Hal, for one. He broke into your garage a couple of times. I suspect he was looking for something in your father's files. He removed a couple of boxes each time he entered."

"Ha! He never bothered to close the door when he left. I kept wondering what was so interesting about my garage!"

"Yes, that was Hal. He was being blackmailed—and the payoff was his stepdaughter. Smart. She already didn't care for him and was causing major issues in his marriage, but he couldn't let anything happen to her, or life as he knew it was over. Plus, he cared about her. He was not the threat we were looking for. He's not involved with drugs that we can tell. He was just a pawn, a means to an end. I don't think you would have even known anything was going on with the garage if he had been more careful. I suspect he thought he could explain himself to you if you caught him, which you almost did when Abigail Rose followed him into the garage."

"You knew that much detail? You knew I could be in danger and never said a word to me? What kind of coldhearted bastard are you?" she asked angrily. At that remark, Mark looked embarrassed. "So, who started the garage on fire? That doesn't sound like Hal. Whoever set my garage on fire had something more in mind."

"It wasn't Hal. When we were alerted to someone on the premises, two of us rushed over. We never saw his face, but his physique was taller, beefier. At least we stopped him from setting your house on fire. He saw us coming and took off in the other direction. We couldn't catch up with him, and we wanted to be sure you were okay."

"Who is 'we'?"

"We've had three agents on the beach. Two of them stayed in the Gallagher cabin. And, of course, I was there," he said sheepishly.

"And who is 'he'?" she pressed on.

"You aren't going to like the answer," he responded cautiously.

She raised her eyebrows as she studied his reaction. "Oh, no, no, no, no, no . . ."

"It's your new friend. We've had him under surveillance for a long time."

Carley put her head in her hands, tears threatening to overwhelm her. "How could I be so stupid? How could I so misread him?"

Mark patted her shoulder in a protective way. "Don't blame yourself. He's smooth. He's gotten away with a lot more than this by using his charm."

It was too much to comprehend. Carley felt like her world had been turned upside down.

"There's more," he said cautiously.

"*More?*" she asked disbelievingly.

Mark looked her carefully in the eye. "We think your father was dragged into this conspiracy."

"He would never have been part of something so devious. You didn't know him—he was a wonderful man, one of the most honest and brilliant men I've ever known. He never would have done anything even remotely unethical, much less something that would put the people he loved at risk."

"I know that," Mark said. "We think he found out about Hal and confronted him. Most likely, your father threatened to tell the authorities what he knew. Because his focus was on home-made bombs, he had access to large amounts of volatile chemicals in his research. When some of it disappeared, he began to suspect something was amiss. Hal wasn't a bad man—he was just a vulnerable target."

"Lithium," she repeated. "UPS brought a delivery addressed to my father just a few days ago. It was lithium."

Now it was Mark's turn to be surprised. "That explains one piece of the puzzle. Lithium is a controlled substance, and I'm sure your father was approved to handle it. I imagine the shipping firm didn't know he was deceased and someone else was placing the orders using his name."

Carley was stunned. It was so much information to process. She was devastated at the thought of all her father had dealt with alone. It made some sense to her. Her father wasn't young when he died, but he wasn't old either at sixty-seven. He had been in great physical condition, and it was a shock when he'd had a heart attack. The stress of what was transpiring must have pushed him over the edge.

"Things are happening, and I don't want you caught in the crosshairs of what's going down. We're about to move on Lindsey. We're fairly sure we know where she is. We had monitored every abandoned building in a fifty-mile radius for the past several weeks but hadn't retried the storage units until you said you had heard a noise coming from one of them. Now we know where they've been moving her around. We've had a SWAT team in position all morning."

Carley reeled from that information. She had been so close and so unsuspecting. The poor girl. Hopefully she was still alive. Mark seemed to think she was, but he also knew that time was running out.

"I've got one more question for you. Last night, someone tried to break into my lake home. Were you aware of that? They weren't successful because Abigail scared them off."

Mark looked somber. "No," he said. "Our attention was on the girl."

"Great," Carley remarked with some dismay.

35

Looking online, she found a law firm in Fargo that had a patent attorney on staff, a woman named Leslie Walker. Checking her bio, Carley found they had graduated from the same high school, Leslie about six years earlier than she. Her credentials looked strong, so Carley immediately contacted her office. Her assistant was able to work Carley in right away.

When Leslie walked into the office, Carley was impressed. She was a tall, slightly more wholesome version of Lauren Bacall—beautiful, smart, well dressed, with very high-heeled shoes. Carley laughed to herself. She could kill herself trying to wear shoes like that, but she thought they probably came in useful when Leslie was trying to impress a jury or a corporate product development team. Carley laid out the documents from her father's files. After riffling through the papers, Leslie pulled out one document that she studied intently.

"This is primarily what I need. I'll do some more research to find out what the status of the patent is and what other, similar patents have been filed. After I learn more, you and I should meet to lay out a plan for dealing with the university and others who may have patents to ensure there hasn't been any infringement. If we find anything of interest, you may want to loop your brother into a future meeting, since he owns half of the interest on these patents. Let me get through step one first, though."

Carley felt certain she had made a good choice of attorneys to represent her and John. She should probably let her brother know what she was doing. It would be an expensive process, but she felt it was important to make sure their ducks were in a row.

Running a few errands while she was still in Fargo, Carley was surprised to get a phone call from Leslie only a couple of hours after she left her office.

"Hi there. I had my assistant get started on this project. He found that an addendum had been filed for your father's patent two years ago. Did you know about that? Your father turned the rights of the patent over to someone else. You told me your father died about then. Can you tell me the actual date of his death?"

"He died on March 8, two years ago this spring. Do you need a copy of his death certificate? And when was the addendum signed?" Carley asked.

"Yes, I'd like a copy of his death certificate. The addendum was signed on March 7. That seems like interesting timing, given that he had already named the patents in his will. I suppose he didn't have time to adjust his will. However, I will have his signature analyzed to make sure there hasn't been any forgery. I have a copy of his signature on the patent application. Do I have your permission to go ahead and verify it?"

"Of course," Carley replied, slightly overwhelmed by the strangeness of this news.

It was several hours before her phone rang again. Leslie told her, "I have some information for you. The patent has been transferred to a Hal Johnson. Do you know him?"

Carley was completely caught off guard. *Hal Johnson.* Why Hal? Perhaps he'd had conversations with Dean Anderson about taking over his father's work. But couldn't he have done that without the patent transfer? Was it just a coincidence that transfer happened the day before her father died? And did the dean know? Perhaps she needed to find that out.

"I have one other odd piece of information." Leslie interrupted Carley's head spinning. "Your father's signature appears to be made by the same person who applied for the patent. In the patent application, his signature is Arthur G. Norgren. But in the signature to transfer the patent to Hal Johnson, the signature reads Arthur D. Norgren Jr. Did your father have two middle names? And was he named after his father? Did he use *Jr.* as a suffix?"

Carley felt totally befuddled. "His middle name was George. I can't think of any reason he would use *D*. Same with *Jr*. He wasn't a junior; his father's name was Wallace. Does *Jr.* mean anything in patent lingo? Or in the chemical field? He was a PhD. I never heard him use the initials *JR* for any reason."

Leslie said, "I don't know why he would use *Jr.* if he wasn't Arthur G. Norgren II."

Carley stammered, "I don't know what to make of any of this right now. I'll contact the dean to see if he knows what it might mean and what his understanding of Hal's connection to the patent is. I'll get back to you."

36

There was static in the air, and Carley was aware of cars coming and going on the dirt road leading to her cabin. The road had been barricaded, so lake residents had to come in the back way. She wished she could watch the action from a distance and be of some help. A girl's life was at stake. It seemed surreal, especially here.

It was midafternoon. The SWAT team had been in place for almost six hours. They were getting tired, despite their rigorous training to withstand almost any resistance. Until there was movement outside the storage unit, they wouldn't risk advancing. The mosquitoes and black flies were annoying, but none of SWAT team members were willing to leave their posts. While they were getting tired of hiding in the cornfield, there was no other choice. The life of a sixteen-year-old girl depended on their agility.

The storage unit, at the top of a hill adjacent to the trucking business, had ten large, garage-like, windowless stalls. Attention was focused on two in particular. One was where three men had been seen coming and going. The other was where they thought the girl was being held. Their listening equipment had not detected the girl's voice for some time. They hoped that was because the men just weren't talking with her, not because she couldn't talk or had been moved again. They could only hope their earlier intelligence was correct.

They were fairly certain there were only three men on the premises. Carefully, the SWAT team, dressed in Ghillie suits to camouflage their appearance, slid like snakes on their stomachs through the tall vegetation until there were five snipers in front of the storage unit, five in back, and two on either end. They were not going to let these men get by them. An FBI Hostage Rescue Team stood just outside of view. It was a seasoned group from Chicago who had experience with situations involving kidnap victims. Their primary goal was to get her out alive, but they also needed to get information about who all was involved. Was it just these three, or were there other people pulling strings behind the scenes?

Two of the SWAT team members made it to the front door of the first unit. For what seemed like an eternity, they stood next to the door of the building, their backs against the wall, waiting for one of the men to come out. Finally, they were rewarded. As a man emerged with a cigarette in hand, the two SWAT team members simultaneously tasered and hit him with a 40 mm "less lethal" launcher designed to knock him down, not kill him. It worked, and the thug crumpled to the ground. Two other SWAT team members rushed forward, grabbing the man under his arms and dragging him to the road, where a van appeared and opened its door, swallowing him up.

About twenty minutes later, another man came out looking for the first one. He had a gun in a holster over his shoulder, just like a cowboy in an old western. As he started to call out the first man's name, two SWAT team members again stepped forward, tasered him and used the 40mm launcher, catapulting him to the ground. Unfortunately, he yelled out just as he was hit. This meant trouble. There was another man in the unit. If the two storage units were connected, and it was likely that they were, it meant that the girl could be in great danger. Instinctively, the FBI HRT burst into the unit with others following quickly on their heels. Exploding two "flash-bangs" into the unit to disorient the man, they jumped into the room, guns drawn.

It was too late. The man had grabbed his gun and then the girl, pointing his gun at her head. The girl, still chained to a chair, looked terrified. Several SWAT team members had their weapons aimed at the man.

"Don't be crazy," the SWAT team leader advised. "We've got you surrounded. There are twenty officers in the vicinity. You're not getting out of here alive if you pull that trigger."

"I'm walking out of here now or the girl dies," the armed man blustered. With that, he cocked his gun to prove he meant it.

"Just calm down, calm down. We don't want to hurt you. We just want Lindsey. Let her go, and we can make this go away."

"I don't believe you. You don't give a crap about either of us," the man with the gun replied.

"Tell us why you did it," the SWAT team leader explained calmly. "We want to understand."

"I didn't do it. Neither did these other two. We were hired to take care of the girl. That's all we did."

"Hired by whom?" the SWAT team leader queried.

"I'm not saying until you get me out of here."

"You're not the one we want. We want the mastermind. Talk to us. We can make you a deal. You can get out of here alive."

The man with a gun looked like a trapped animal. He was getting more and more agitated, which concerned the SWAT team. One wrong move or one overreaction from him and it could be all over for the girl.

"You back out now, or she dies!" the gunman shouted. He was struggling to come up with a plan. This wasn't what they'd rehearsed. And they were so close to the end. He'd have to scare them away.

"We can help you here," the SWAT team leader continued calmly. "We'll take good care of you. But you have to cooperate with us." He took a step toward the gunman.

"Stop there!" the gunman said emphatically. With that, he adjusted the gun pointed at the girl's head for emphasis. "You won't help me. It's only the girl you want."

"Not true. I'm saying it again. You are not our target. We need to find out who is behind all this. Why is the girl being held? If you know what's good for you, you'll help us now."

"I'm telling you, get out. I'm not your pawn. If you want this girl to live, you'll get me a car. And you'll let us walk out of here without any trouble. If you don't, the girl dies."

"I'll see what I can do. Let me contact my supervisor to let him know what you need." As the SWAT team leader reached for his radio, the gunman aimed his gun at the SWAT leader's head as if to make sure he didn't say anything out of line. It was a big mistake. Believing he might shoot him or the girl, one of the officers, whose AR-15 was aimed at the man's head, shot him in the temple. The clean hit caused the man's head to explode as if it were a water balloon.

The young girl, covered with blood and bits of flesh, jumped away from the bloody mess, screaming at the top of her lungs in total disbelief, not able to fully understand what had just happened. One of the SWAT team raced over to her, wrapped his arms around her, and pulled her away from the body. It took the men some time to find the key to the lock in the jeans pocket of the corpse to unlock the chain that held her. With terror in her eyes, the girl sobbed while they worked to unchain her. At last, she was free. One of the SWAT team members brought a blanket to wrap around her. She leaned into his shoulder, sobbing uncontrollably.

"It's okay," he said. "It's okay. You're safe now. Are you okay? Are you in any pain?"

The girl shook her head. Still confused, she hesitated.

"Can you walk?" the SWAT team leader asked her gently.

She nodded silently. Still shaking from all that had just happened, she could hardly believe she was free.

It was finally over.

37

As Carley lay in bed that night, she struggled to comprehend all she'd learned. The girl was safe. What a relief that was. It would take Lindsey a long time to get over what had happened, but she was alive. Carley couldn't imagine how relieved Hal must feel. But why in the world did they kidnap her in the first place? Were they ever going to let her go? Why were they keeping her? It was just all so hard to comprehend. Was the FBI certain there were other people involved? And how did Hal fit in?

She felt for Hal. He was in a no-win situation. Lindsey already hated him. If he had something to do with her abduction, she guessed it would be the end of his relationship with his step-daughter and with his wife as well. Of course, it would be hard to maintain that relationship from prison anyway. What did Hal know? Why hadn't he come forward with more information? Why had he deceived her with the lithium? So, who started the garage on fire? That didn't seem like Hal. Whoever did it had something more in mind. Was it Gordon? Mark Dolan had intimated that. But why?

And what was the relationship of Hal to her dad's work?

Despite the swirling thoughts raging in her head, Carley was exhausted by all that had happened that day. She quickly drifted off to sleep.

At around 2:00 a.m., she was awakened by the rumble of trucks nearby. It struck her as odd that the semis were on the move so much in the middle of the night. It was too early for the harvest season, so they weren't carrying crops that had just been picked. What were they carrying?

Suddenly, Carley found herself standing next to her bed. *That's it*, she thought. *Somehow, these trucks are involved. It could be drugs.* It had to be something with a huge payoff—big enough to risk kidnapping a girl and facing the charges that would come along with that. What else could be so valuable to risk so much?

She grabbed her jeans and put them on over the long T-shirt she had worn to bed. Scooping up her cell phone and wallet, she hunted for her car keys. Abigail looked like she couldn't figure out what was going on. Was it time for a walk? Time to play? She nervously followed closely by Carley's heels.

"Not now, girl," Carley admonished. "Go lie down in your bed."

Abigail hung her head and moved slowly toward her bed and looked back at Carley questioningly.

"I mean it. Go lie down."

With that, Abigail jumped into her dog bed, slowly lying down, giving Carley the forlornest look she could.

"I'll be back in a little while," Carley said reassuringly.

As she headed to the back door, she called Mark, who answered groggily.

"Where are you?" she asked.

"I'm at my cabin. Where are you? What's going on? Why are you calling me so late?" Mark asked.

"I'll be at your cabin in two minutes. Be ready. We're going for a little drive."

* * *

As Mark climbed into the car, he smiled at Carley and said, "Playing Nancy Drew, are we?"

"Don't be glib. There's something I want you to see. It woke me up, and it's odd enough I think you should know it's going on."

She drove her sports coupe over the hill and down the dirt road until she came near the crest. She turned off her car lights and slowly inched ahead. About half a mile away, a semi was pulling out of the truck farmer's yard. Another was revved up and ready to roll out.

"I can't imagine why these trucks are leaving now. I heard them last night too. I've never heard them during the day. Only at night."

"There are a lot of reasons truckers leave at this time of day. The traffic is much easier. A lot of them will drive all night and sleep through the day. That doesn't necessarily mean anything," Mark responded.

"But I think it does. Something just doesn't feel right about it. What are the trucks carrying? Sand from the gravel pit? Then who loaded it into the trucks tonight? I think they're carrying something much more valuable."

Mark stared at her intently. "For this you got me out of bed?"

"Yes, and I think you'd better call someone and have them stop the trucks."

"It doesn't work like that. I have to get a warrant. And I couldn't have you with me. If something were going down, you're a civilian, and your life could be in danger."

"All right, all right. I'll go back. But please, will you do what you can? Why can the highway patrol stop me without a warrant but not the criminals?"

"First, we don't know they're criminals yet. They could be moving grain. This is farm country. Second, I'm not highway patrol. But, okay, I'll see what I can do."

With that, they backed up and turned around; Carley dropped Mark off at the cabin where he was staying. He watched from a distance to make sure she made it safely back to hers.

38

The next morning at 7:30, there was a knock on Carley's door. She reached over to the alarm clock, holding it up to see what time it was. Abigail let out a couple of small barks, but Abigail hadn't had much sleep either, and she wasn't making a move off the bed. Carley put on her well-worn terry cloth bathrobe and made her way to the door. As the knock became more insistent, Carley moaned, "I'm coming. I'm coming."

Behind the door, Mark Dolan waited impatiently. He had a lot on his plate today, but this was one loop he wanted to close. Carley was surprised to see him but eagerly invited him in for a cup of coffee.

She sat down at the big oak table across from Mark, who smiled at her, a little paternalistically, she thought.

"Blueprint machines," he mused.

"What?" Carley looked at him curiously.

"You heard me. Blueprint machines. The trucks were carrying blueprint machines."

"I didn't know blueprint machines were even used anymore. I thought everything had gone to CAD," Carley puzzled.

"It doesn't matter what's happening in the printing industry; the trucks were carrying blueprint machines and anhydrous ammonia, which is used for making blueprints. It's all being shipped to architectural firms in New York City and Georgia."

Carley felt sheepish. But he had had the trucks checked out. That impressed her. She didn't think he would. "Oh," was all she could muster.

"Thanks for the wake-up call last night. So glad I could return the favor this morning." Mark winked at her. "I'd better get to the office because you can't be too careful with blueprint machines on the loose."

Carley punched him in the arm.

"Hey, be careful. I could get you arrested for that," Mark quipped.

"Just try," Carley dared him. And she handed him a big blueberry muffin and a cup of coffee in a thermal cup. "For the road."

39

Abigail Rose sat squarely in front of Carley looking forlorn, tail anxiously wagging. Carley burst out laughing. "Subtle, very subtle." She chuckled. With that, she grabbed Abigail's leash and headed out the door with the eager dog. They made their way down the road, with Abigail stopping to sniff every bush along the way.

It was Sunday night, and because most people from the beach were gone, Carley removed Abigail's collar and threw her ball, hoping to wear her out before they got back. Abigail dutifully raced after the ball, caught it, and brought it back expectantly. They continued the ball throwing for another ten minutes. Suddenly, the ball hit a rock in the road and veered off to the left. Abigail followed it into the yard, saw a squirrel, and began to chase it.

Carley followed Abigail into the yard. Realizing there were people in the lake home, she resisted calling out to Abigail. It was dusk, and she didn't want to startle anyone. Plus, she was too tired to have to engage in conversation with anyone.

Through the sheer curtains in the kitchen, she could see the face of the man who was laughing. It was Hank Larson, the owner of the trucking firm. Hank was a large, big-boned man with a rough demeanor and stained hands. He had grown up on the farm where his trucking firm now resided. He had a renter who still planted some of his fields, but acres were taken up by the parked semis and mounds of parts he used to refurbish them. He owned a few trucks of his own, subcontracting with the turkey producer in town and other trucking firms when they needed extra trucks.

Sitting at the round, rough table with him were three other men she didn't recognize. And one she did. Gordon. They were playing poker and smoking cigars, and their conversation was animated.

Suddenly, booming laughter erupted from inside the cabin. "Arthur must be rolling over in his grave," a deep voice boomed. And other voices joined him in laughter.

Her father's name hung in the air like a flashing neon sign. Slowly she retreated, struggling to figure out where she was. *Whose place is this?* she thought. *The attorney's?* It couldn't be her father they were talking about. Did they even know him? It must be someone else they meant.

In the meantime, Abigail had lost interest in the squirrel and had returned, panting, to Carley's feet. Scooping her up, Carley quietly soothed her, finding her way back to the road. She wanted to eavesdrop near the window but was afraid someone would see her.

Gordon. He was there. So, he was back and wasn't in touch with her. Her whole body went stiff with surprise. But where was his fancy sports car? It wasn't parked in the driveway. There were four cars, however, and she assumed one of them had to be his. Or perhaps someone else had brought him there. He might not have wanted her to see him drive by. Quickly she reached for her cell phone to snap a picture of the plates. It wasn't in her pocket. What a time to have forgotten it. She tried to memorize the four license plates on the cars. Easier said than done.

When Carley got home, she grabbed a pen and paper and wrote down as much as she could remember of the license plates. She could remember two in their entirety, but only parts of the other two. It seemed hopeless. She could go back to get the other two, but she didn't want anyone to see her. Calling Mark, she left a message that she had spotted Gordon and that they should talk.

40

When her cell phone rang early the next morning, Carley was startled to see Mac's name come up. *Oh, damn*, she thought. *I don't want to talk to you. Why are you calling me now?*

Reluctantly, she answered the phone. "Hello?"

"Hey," he answered. "How're you doing?"

"Well enough. To what do I owe the pleasure of this call?"

"No chitchat. I understand. I'm coming up to Fargo on business and wondered if I could stop by. I could drop off the boxes for you."

What was she expecting? Did she think he missed her? Of course. The boxes. They must be in his way. Her heart still raced when she heard his voice, but it was a combination of hurt, anger, and embarrassment. She had gotten over loving him, even though she hadn't really gotten over life without him. She was still winding her way through that. Gordon had been a great diversion until he betrayed her. Now what was he up to?

"Sure. I forgot about the boxes. What day? What time?"

"Well, probably Tuesday around noon. How does that look for you? We could go out for lunch if you can spare the time."

Ha, she thought. *Let me check my hectic schedule.* But she responded, "Tuesday will work. We can meet at the café at the bait shop."

"Does that mean we have to eat worms?" He laughed.

"Very funny," she said dryly. "You've been there before. Remember the place with the great burgers?"

"Oh yeah. I liked it. Pretty down-home. But that's fine. Why don't I pick you up?"

"That's okay. I'll meet you there. I have to go into Detroit Lakes after that. See you then," she said, bringing the conversation to a close. She had nothing else to say to him.

41

On Tuesday, Carley awoke feeling unsettled. She didn't really want to see Mac. She knew she needed to be an adult and retrieve her boxes, but she hardly cared about whatever stuff he still had, and seeing him was painful, especially knowing this was just a transaction. She lay in bed contemplating her options. Correctly assessing she didn't have many, she decided she'd better get up and get dressed. She wondered what she should wear. Jeans and a T-shirt? Jeans and a sexy top? Finally, she settled on jeans and a respectable, V-neck shirt. She wasn't going to try too hard to impress Mac.

By 11:50 a.m., she was at the bait shop. There was a fine line between being on time and appearing overeager. Mac texted her that he'd had to make a stop in Fergus Falls and would be about ten minutes late. She walked up and down a couple of aisles, looking aimlessly at tackle and fishing supplies while her stomach did flip-flops. Glancing at her watch, she walked to the restaurant in the back of the building. The diner was stuck in the '70s with red plastic cushions, Formica-topped tables, and waitresses in red gingham check server outfits with white aprons. Mac was just approaching the back door. *He is as darling as ever*, she thought with some chagrin. His eyes always drew her in.

With a deep breath, she walked over to him. "Hi there. You made it."

Smiling at her, Mac said, "Hey. It's good to see you. How've you been?" He gave her a quick hug.

She felt completely flummoxed by how to answer him. Should she admit she'd been totally lost without him? No. Should she admit she had been sucked in by someone who was married? No. Should she tell him she felt completely at loose ends? No.

"I'm fine," she lied. "How about you?"

"Things have been going fairly well. Here, let's get a table."

The waitress led them to a booth in the back. Mac seemed uneasy, but Carley didn't feel like making him more at ease. *He should feel uncomfortable*, she thought.

"So, how's life up here at the lake? Are you enjoying it?" Mac asked.

"Yeah, it's good. It's been more eventful than I had planned, but I'm getting used to it."

"Eventful? How so?"

"For starters, my garage burned down. Actually, someone burned my garage down. They haven't figured out why yet, but someone started the fire after pouring gasoline all around the garage and the house."

"Oh my gosh. Were you hurt? Did the house burn? Did you lose much?"

"The entire thing burned to the ground. I salvaged a few nostalgic things, but almost everything was lost. The house is fine. I'm fine."

"Why would someone do that? Or do they think it might be kids?"

"They don't know. There wasn't much of value. Mostly my father's records, and I think I have a way to retrieve some of those. How about you? How's softball?" Inwardly, she hoped that might make him squirm. It didn't.

"It's good. The playoffs for the championship are next week. Work has been busy." He paused. "Your father's records? Like his research? That could be a big loss."

"The university has most of the original documents. Someone came by to document what they didn't have, so I think I'll be okay there."

"I never thought you totally understood what value you have in his research. Have you checked it out yet? This could be a big deal."

She hated that he was taking such an authoritative tone with her. "I've had a recent conversation with the dean. Aren't you glad this isn't your concern anymore?" She smiled at him demurely.

He flushed. She'd made her point. But he pressed on, "If I were you, I'd make sure you had someone go over it all with you in depth. Maybe you'll have time for that now."

"Well, I certainly must have more time on my hands now, with you out of the picture. Is that what you're saying?"

"I just meant you're so close to Fargo now it would be easier than it was when you lived in Minneapolis."

"I'm sure you'll be surprised to know I'm building a life here, and I'm busier than you might expect."

Not liking the direction this conversation was taking, Mac said, "I've got your boxes in my car. There are five of them. They're heavy. You must have a collection of rocks and books! I can transfer them to your car when we're done. Or, if you don't have enough room in your car, I can bring them to your cabin."

That was the last thing she wanted: Mac on her home turf. "That's okay. I emptied out the back of my car. We can put them there."

The silence that ensued was uncomfortable. They had been lovers for three years. How could they have nothing to talk about now?

"I'm sorry I hurt you," Mac admitted. "I never meant to do that."

"That's good to hear," she said matter-of-factly.

"I miss you. Is there a chance we could still be friends?" he asked wistfully.

"I have a hard time picturing that."

"Things just happened. Sometimes I wish they hadn't."

"Thanks," she said without much emotion. "Me too."

"This is harder than I'd expected. I'd really like to be friends. I miss you."

She stared at his earnest face and pleading eyes. "What about your new flame? Isn't she still in the picture?"

"Kristin? Well, yes, she's still around."

Carley sat there dumbfounded. "And you thought what? Kristin wouldn't mind if you and I were friends? Carley must be so desperate she'll go along with anything? What the hell are you thinking? What kind of friendship do you think we can have?" She couldn't believe what he was asking of her.

"I don't know. It just seems too bad that everything we had has to go away."

"I can't do this," she choked. She rose from her seat. "Let's skip lunch and get the boxes. I need to get out of here."

Mac jumped to his feet and followed her out to the parking lot. This hadn't gone at all the way he'd hoped.

42

That evening, Carley took Abigail Rose for a walk as she contemplated all that had happened over the past couple of days. Her conversation with Mac had hit her hard. They had been so good together, it was hard to let that go. She knew he still cared about her, but caring and commitment are two different things.

Lindsey was free, and it was—at least in part—because she'd told Mark she had heard mewing near a storage unit. What if she hadn't mentioned that? It certainly didn't seem like anything to her, certainly not that it was related to the girl at all. It was smart of Lindsey to have mewed in the first place, but she shuddered at how that little piece of information could have been so easily overlooked. Her estimation of Mark had risen considerably.

The sun was just going down, the lake still brightly lit in the sunset. This was her favorite time of day, with a sense of anticipation, of centering, of quieting down, and she loved it. She tended to go full steam ahead most of the time, so this space in the day was always precious to her. Lost in her own thoughts, she hadn't paid much attention to where she and Abigail were walking.

Suddenly, she was aware that they were nearing the cabin where she had seen Gordon. Four cars were again in the driveway. No, this time, it was five. She started to turn on her heel and head back to her own cabin. She didn't want to risk bumping into Gordon. What would she say to him? Why didn't he call her after he returned from the conference? Why didn't he tell her he had a wife? Was he responsible for her garage fire? It was too much to process. What kind of a man was he?

Then she had a change of heart. Instead of heading back home, she pulled her cell phone, which at least she had remembered to bring this time, out of her pocket. Ambling back by the lawyer's lake home, she unobtrusively took photos of the three remaining license plate numbers.

When she returned to her cabin, her neck was tightening up as it always did when she was under stress. She could feel a headache coming on, and she hardly ever got headaches. Despite that, she jotted down the three new license plate numbers with a sense of satisfaction, adding them to the other two she had gotten the previous day.

Why hadn't Gordon told her he knew people down the beach? There was something so disconcerting knowing he was in the area. Did one of the cars belong to him? She had to know.

Searching online, she found a website where, for only $19.95, she could have a one-month subscription to license plate lookups. She couldn't resist. The first two numbers were no surprise: Henry Larson and Jude Parker. Henry—Hank—Larson she knew. He was the truck farmer. Jude Parker was the attorney who owned the cabin where the men were gathering, the attorney whose wife went missing and was never found. The next two names weren't familiar: William McCoy and James Reston. Further searching, she discovered William McCoy was a business owner in the area. His company, Manufacturtek, distributed industrial products used in manufacturing plants.

When she pulled up information about James Reston, her heart stopped. James Reston was Gordon Locklear. He had a PhD in chemical engineering. The picture that appeared was about ten years old and was from an old university website when he was an assistant professor. No wonder Helen had been so sure Gordon was still in Europe. He was. James Reston, however, wasn't. She could feel the earth shifting under her feet.

When she pulled up the fifth name, she choked. Without thinking, she jumped to her feet, gave a treat to Abigail, and grabbed two beers from the refrigerator. Locking the door behind her, she headed to Mark's cabin. It was 9:30 now, and she hoped he was there.

A surprised Mark Dolan answered the door. "Well, I wasn't expecting company. To what do I owe the pleasure of this visit? It must be serious because you brought reinforcements."

"It is," she said as she handed Mark a beer. "Are you going to keep me standing out here, or can I come in?"

"By all means, come in. I feel honored. Remember you're entering a bachelor pad where the man in question wasn't expecting company."

"I don't care what your place looks like. I need to talk to you. I have a really bad feeling about something."

With that, Mark led Carley into the sparsely decorated living room, where he had papers spread out all over and a few dirty dishes on an end table.

"What gives?" he asked.

"I can't quite put the pieces together, but I keep finding pieces, and I thought maybe you could."

"Well, I'll give it my best shot. Try me."

"When I was out walking Abigail the night before last, I had her off leash. I know, I'm a bad person. I was throwing a ball for her as we walked, and suddenly a squirrel caught her attention, and she darted off into the yard we were passing. There were four cars parked there and a group of men inside. When I got closer to the cabin to intercept Abigail, one of the men said, 'Arthur must be rolling over in his grave.' You may not know this, but there aren't many Arthurs in the world, and my father was one of them. It just seemed like a very odd comment. I didn't stick around long because I didn't want them to see me, so Abigail and I hightailed it out of there. But first, I got two of the license plate numbers of the four cars. I felt kind of silly about that. You can call me Nancy Drew again. I didn't do anything about that right away. Memorizing four plates was harder than I expected, so I guess I'm a bad Nancy Drew. Then, today, when I walked Abigail again near the same cabin, there were the same cars plus one more."

"I take it you went home tonight and looked up who those license plates belonged to, am I right?" Mark queried.

"Yes. And the results surprised me. Of course, Jude Parker, the attorney who owns the cabin, was one of the names of the car owners. No surprise there. But the others were all a surprise."

"Let me guess—Hank Larson, the truck farmer, was another one."

"Yes. Hank Larson was there. Is he one of the reasons you're on the beach? And Gordon, well, Gordon isn't Gordon, I discovered. His name is James Reston, and he used to be on the faculty with my dad as an assistant professor about ten years ago from the looks of it. I found an old picture of him at the university. I knew everyone else in the picture."

Mark looked startled. "We knew that was his name. I didn't know you didn't. Whom did the other two belong to?"

Startled by the fact that he knew who Gordon really was, she continued, "William McCoy was one. Do you know him?"

"I've heard of him, but not connected with what's going on around here. Who is he?"

"He's the CEO and owner of Manufacturtek. His company distributes industrial products for manufacturing plants. But I found a product on his website that was interesting—a spectrometer. You know, that's what my dad's research was about. He was designing a small, portable unit that could be used in a wide range of applications, including transportation—evaluating the chemical content of liquids being transported. The Department of Defense was interested because of potential terrorism applications.

The one I found on the website was remarkably similar. It isn't common technology, and my father held all the patents for such a device. And who do you think the last person was?" Carley asked.

"It surprised you, didn't it?"

"Absolutely. It was the biggest surprise of all. Give?"

Mark chuckled. It felt reassuring to her. "Come on, stop with the suspense. You're killing me!"

"Tom Bradshaw."

"Tom Bradshaw, the sheriff?" Mark exclaimed.

"The one and only. I wasn't expecting that at all."

"Wow. That's very interesting—a star-studded cast. Of course, we can't prove this group has done anything wrong just because they said Arthur won't like it. They could be a poker group. And what could be making Arthur roll over in his grave is someone getting stung by a good bluff. Hal has alluded that a regular poker game is how they got to know each other."

"Well, they may be poker buddies, but they also have a lot of odd things that connect them. One of them is distributing a portable spectrometer like the one my father developed. Another wanted to get the research from my dad's file cabinet in the garage but lied about who he was. The third had storage units adjacent to his property where the kidnapped girl was being held. The attorney, well, I'm not sure what he's doing there. But the sheriff? He never reported the two incidents he came out to my lake home for—the garage break-in and the garage burning down. And the comment, 'Arthur must be rolling in his grave,' must mean my dad wouldn't have liked what's going on."

"So, you think they're in cahoots together?" Mark asked.

"I think they are. Maybe Jude handles all the legal issues for the business. That would make some sense. But what if they're using my dad's patents? Did you know that my dad transferred ownership of the patents to Hal just before he died? I just don't get that. They were important enough for him to list them in his will. I hired a patent attorney to check it out, and she's doing some work on that right now. She said the signatures weren't an exact match on the patent application and the patent reassignment. She's having a handwriting specialist research whether they were signed by the same person. But, on the reassignment of the patent to Hal, he signed his name Arthur D. Norgren Jr. His middle initial is *G*, not *D*, and he never used a *D* in his signature, much less *Jr.*"

"Was he a junior? Was he named after his dad?"

"No. That's what makes it so strange. There's another thing that's struck me. My father's spectrometer was designed specifically for the transportation industry. But remember, it was funded in part by the Department of Defense, who wanted to be able to quickly identify if there were risks of homemade bombs in trucks or shipping cargo. It made me think again about the trucks leaving Hank's farm with anhydrous ammonia."

"Ah yes. The very frightening blueprint machines."

"Okay, you're mocking me. But look at this." With that, Carley pulled out a large piece of the metal from the bag she had rescued from the lake. "Could this be part of a blueprint machine?"

Mark furrowed his brow, turning the metal over and over. "You found this? Where?"

"At the bottom of the lake. I was out kayaking one night and didn't turn my lights on. Again, just shoot me. But I watched three men push a big bag off a pontoon. I reported that to the sheriff too, but—now that I think about it—I'm fairly certain he never did anything about that, either. I went back early one morning and pulled it out."

"I remember the night you were kayaking. I was watching you."

"That's creepy," Carley commented dryly. "I think you enjoy that part of your job."

Mark flushed. "You're probably right. Just trying to keep tabs on things on the beach. It's a tough job, but someone's got to do it," he quipped, smiling.

Ignoring his fun at her expense, she continued, "And what about the lithium that was delivered to my garage? Where has that ended up?"

He stared at her dumbfounded. "You think it's in the trucks, don't you?"

"Well, it has to be somewhere, right?"

"So that would mean they have anhydrous ammonia and lithium in the same trucks. That can't be good. That's the stuff of homemade bombs. Why would they be carrying that? We'd better find those damn trucks."

With that, Mark jumped up from his chair, grabbed his cell phone, and quickly started pushing buttons.

"Ralph. It's Mark. We need to get to those trucks again. I know, I know. It's something we didn't anticipate. We're looking for lithium hidden in the blueprint machines. Figure out where it's hidden and call me back." With that, Mark hung up.

"I think I need that beer now," he said.

43

Mark gave Carley a quick hug and told her he would take her home and she should wait for his call. Reaching into his glove compartment, he pulled out a small revolver and a box of bullets, asking, "Could you use this if you had to?"

She choked at the thought of how real the danger was. The gun was smaller than the one she had used at the shooting range. She nodded tentatively.

He showed her how to hold it, how to load it, how to aim it. "It won't do you any good to have it if you can't shoot it."

"I can do it," she said, not sure if she was trying to convince him or herself.

She really wanted to join him in the search of the trucks, but she understood the liability. It was nearly 10:00 as he pulled into her driveway to drop her off. Inside, Abigail and Prattle were asleep, each barely noticing when she walked in the door.

The next morning, Carley found it impossible to concentrate. While she had some work to finish on her project, she just couldn't wrap her mind around it. She wanted to talk with Mark to find out what he'd learned, but she was certain he would get in touch with her when there was something he felt she should know.

A knock on her door broke her reverie. When she reached the doorway, she called out to the person on the other side, not wanting to open the door. However, she was pleasantly surprised by who was on the other side. It was the Realtor, Jeff Barnes. Pulling open the door, she asked, "So, do you have an offer for me?"

Jeff looked startled. "Well, yeah, I do. I didn't have your phone number and wondered if you'd like to grab dinner and a movie this Friday night."

Carley started to chuckle. "I'm sorry. It isn't funny. I just meant did you have an offer on my lake home? Remember, you're a Realtor."

Jeff flushed slightly. "Oh, this isn't a business call! And you haven't changed your mind about selling, have you?"

Carley reassured him she hadn't changed her mind, told him she would be happy to go for dinner and a movie, and gave him her cell phone number so he could let her know what time he would pick her up. She was surprised he hadn't forgotten about her. She figured it helped that she was the new girl in town, especially when it was a small town.

When she closed the door after he left, she decided it was nice to have a diversion on the calendar. He seemed nice enough, even though she didn't feel he was quite her type. *Nice* seemed to be the operative word. While she had sworn off men, she didn't think she would ever care about him the way she did about Mac or Gordon. *Nice* had its advantages. Of course, there could be a lot of water over the dam by Friday. After all, it was only Monday now.

She went back to her laptop and tried to get focused. It just wasn't going to happen. As she thought about the trucks moving out, she wondered if she'd let her imagination get away with her. Gordon—or James—wasn't a figment of her imagination. The fire wasn't a figment of her imagination. The lithium delivery wasn't a figment of her imagination. Things were happening all around her. What kind of danger was she in now?

Unable to stand the suspense, Carley put Abigail's leash on her and walked to the end of her driveway where she could see Mark's cabin. There was no car there, so he wasn't back yet. They continued to amble around the yard, Abigail sniffing at bushes.

Carley was afraid to venture any farther. Sitting out on her back deck, she waited for Mark to return.

Finally, around seven o'clock that evening, she was rewarded. Spotting her outside, he pulled into her driveway.

"Well, I have a lot of news for you. You were right about the trucks. It turned out that they not only had blueprint machines, they had lithium and anhydrous ammonia, and were headed to three destinations. Want to hear more?"

"Of course!" Carley chortled.

"At first, the truck drivers said they didn't have any idea what was planned. We were quite sure that wasn't true. When they heard that domestic terrorism charges could be brought against them, one of them started to spill, implicating Hank Larson as not only the owner of the trucks but also as the master organizer of the where they were going. The drivers said they had orders to leave the cargo and rigs in New York City, Chicago, and Chattanooga and set timers once everything was in place. Two detonations were planned in densely populated areas and one at the intersection of two major highways just outside Chattanooga that would cripple transportation from the north and south."

"You mean they were going to hurt hundreds of people? But why?"

"They insisted they had no idea that the trucks were going to be blown up or why. They indicated they have worked for Hank Larson for years. I'm guessing they've probably been part of the drug trafficking that brought me here in the first place," Mark noted. "We're getting the semis tested for drug residue now."

"Why were they detonating explosives in the trucks?" Carley asked, bewildered.

"Their plan was that they would simulate terrorist attacks, then swoop in with a product, a spectrometer, that could give law officials a tool to quickly evaluate liquids to determine their risk. They would sell spectrometers to identify and prevent homemade bombs. They needed a lot of commotion and collateral damage to ensure that the demand for spectrometers would skyrocket. In the end, they would have a legitimate business that would generate millions for each of them."

"And they admitted that?"

"We had some great intel. Once he knew his stepdaughter was safe, Hal began to talk in return for immunity. Initially, Sheriff Bradshaw, Jude Parker, Hank Larson, and William McCoy were all poker buddies of James Reston. The Fab Five. Hal made six. They formed a company that was manufacturing the spectrometers in China that you found on the Manufacturtek website. They all had skin in the game except Hal. Hal didn't have any money to invest, but he did have access to information and chemicals."

"Wait a minute. You gave Hal immunity, even though he was part of this?" Carley asked incredulously.

"Yes. His role was minimal, and he had balked at doing what Reston wanted him to do—blowing up hundreds of people— which is why Reston had Hal's stepdaughter kidnapped to silence him. I figured he had suffered a fair amount already. Plus, his career at the university is ended. Immunity, of course, depends on everything he's told us checking out."

He continued, "Two agents picked up Hank, who immediately lawyered up with Jude Parker. Hank expected him to lock things down. I'm sure he would have; only what Hank didn't expect was that we had a warrant for Jude's arrest as well. Maybe they can share a lawyer." Mark smirked. "Just kidding." Mark became serious again. "All Hank has disclosed so far is that he had a contract to transport the blueprint machines for an unnamed customer. He hasn't produced the contract yet, but he's claiming ignorance."

"What about the storage unit where Lindsey was held? That was on Hank's property," Carley pointed out.

"Yes, he has pointed the finger at the men who held Lindsey captive. He said he didn't know anything about her kidnapping, that they had just rented the storage unit and he had no idea it was going to be used for such a devious purpose. But we know better.

Remember, we have two of Lindsey's kidnappers in custody. It's in their best interests to be on our side now."

"Did you go after William McCoy?" Carley asked.

"William is the most interesting of the bunch. He appears to have the least risk in this plan, yet he's the one who's making the whole sham possible. Without him, the scheme couldn't have worked. So, yes, he's been detained."

"And my friend the sheriff?" Carley pressed.

"The sheriff is being interrogated as we speak. There's enough evidence that he knew all about the kidnapping and explosions. He'll be detained and charged with plans to commit domestic terrorism, along with the others. Because of the charges, none of them will be released on bail.

"There's more," Mark continued, "One of the Minnesota state senators, Michael Langford, sits on the Senate Committee on Commerce, Science, and Transportation. He had introduced a bill to fund spectrometers for every state highway department, and he's a friend of Jude Parker's, so he's in on this somehow."

"How did you find that out?"

"Through our buddy Hal, and one of my friends in the Senate confirmed it. Reston had a major marketing campaign ready to roll out across the US to sell the spectrometer to local police departments as well as Homeland Security."

"There's one person you haven't mentioned," Carley said cautiously.

"That is the bad news. We haven't found Reston, the mastermind, yet. There is a warrant out for his arrest, but he's lying low. Trust me, we'll find him, though it may take a few days. Now for the part that involves you," he finished.

"Me? How could I be involved with this? I don't know anyone except James and Hal, and James lied to me about who he was. How can I possibly be mixed up in this?"

"I didn't say you were 'mixed up in this.' I said that there is part that involves you. When we confronted the group about this scheme, Jude Parker quickly produced a document that showed your father had given his rights to the patents he held to Hal. I know you're aware of that document. Do you really think your father would have willingly done that?"

"I don't know what to think. The attorney I hired questioned his signature. He was a very smart person and shrewd professional. Why would he give away his patents? That was the culmination of his life's work," Carley responded. "And they were named in his will, so I know his original intent was to pass the patents on to my brother and me."

"That's what I thought," Mark admitted. "That leads me to my biggest concern. Your dad was under distress. I know he died here, at Pelican Lake, from a heart attack. Or at least that was the conclusion at the time. Yet you've said he was relatively young—sixty-seven years old—and in very good shape. We think he was forced to sign his patents over to Hal—not by Hal but by James Reston. Reston did that so Hal couldn't talk without implicating himself. He knew Hal was the weak link in his armor. I believe there's a strong likelihood your dad was killed because he stood between Reston and his future profitability. He was angry your father had him fired from the university for ethics violations and determined to get even. We have reason to believe your father was murdered."

With that, Carley felt her legs go weak and her body began to shake. She crumbled into a chair as she let out a choked sob.

Swallowing hard, she said quietly, "I had no idea what he was going through. How did you figure this all out?"

"Partly, it came from Hal."

"From Hal? What did he tell you?"

"He told me Reston had resented your father for years. He blamed him for everything bad that happened to him since he was let go. He went after what your father had built, and things got out of control. He's been spiraling ever since—kidnapping Hal's stepdaughter, planning to explode trucks around the country, and, possibly, killing your father to get access to the rights that could make him a multimillionaire."

"JR!" Carley gasped. "The initials after his signature. James Reston. My dad left us a message."

44

Carley stood with the others huddled near her father's grave site. The cemetery was on the outskirts of Fargo, surrounded by farms and fields. In the distance, she could hear a cow bellowing. It was a penetratingly cold day, even though it was June. *Weather up here is so unpredictable*, she thought as she shivered in her lightweight summer jacket. A storm was brewing, and a cold front was passing through. She felt as if a cold front was passing through her life, and how appropriate it was that it was such a miserable day. She watched in disbelief as the crane moved the earth from the ground.

Five people were with her—Mark, two other FBI agents whom she had just met, someone from the coroner's office, and a representative of the cemetery. For all of them, this was just business. For her, this was a painful, gut-wrenching experience. It was hard enough the first time to bury her father. Having to go through this all again, especially for the reason they were doing it now, made it ten times more difficult.

Mark directed the activity. He was cool and calm as the casket was lifted from the ground. She felt detached from all that was happening. *This is surreal.* She was numb, and she couldn't tell if it was from the cold or shock that her father may have been murdered.

The hydraulic lifter pulled the casket from its cocoon. They slid the casket onto a dolly and gently steered it toward the waiting hearse that would transport it to the coroner's office. She was surprised that the surface of the casket still had its shiny, well-polished wood surface.

Once the casket was in the hearse, the five men shook hands and disbanded. Mark walked over to her.

"How are you doing? Are you okay?" he gently asked.

"I'm alright. My head is pounding. I can't believe what we just did. It's not anything I ever thought I would witness in my lifetime."

"I know. I'm sure it was hard enough the first time around. You've been really brave through all of this. Are you all right with the casket being transported to the morgue? Or do you want to accompany it?"

"I don't want to see him. I want to remember him the way he was the last time we were together—warm, laughing, fun. I'm counting on you to make sure it's my dad and that there aren't any other surprises."

"Don't worry, we'll take care of things from here." With that, Mark escorted Carley to her car. "It will take a few days, but I'll get in touch with you as soon as I know anything."

45

Three days had passed since her father's body had been exhumed. She had expected to hear from Mark by now. She had called her brother, John, in California, to let him know what was happening, but he had decided not to come back for the exhumation. She understood. It felt like digging up all the raw emotion she had experienced with his death. Grief is a powerful force, and she didn't know if she could face it head-on again. Not that it ever really left her. The white-hot images of what her father's body would look like made her shudder. She didn't want to see him; that's not how she wanted to remember him. She was quite sure she might never get over it. Mark had assured her she wouldn't need to witness it.

Suddenly, her cell phone ring broke her reverie. Recognizing Mark's number, her hands began to shake.

"Hello?" Her voice was weak and tentative.

"Hi there. It's Mark. Could I stop by to give you an update? I'm on my way out to the lake now."

"Of course. I'm just waiting here." She knew she would have to steel herself for what was to come.

It felt like hours before Mark arrived, but it was only about twenty-five minutes. When she answered the door, she gave Mark a weak smile, and suddenly she began to weep. Heaving, choking tears flew out of her eyes, startling even her.

"I'm sorry. I wasn't going to do that."

Mark didn't say a word but walked over to her and wrapped his arms around her. She burrowed her head into his shoulder, her body shaking uncontrollably. He held her until her shaking subsided.

"Let's sit down," he said calmly to her.

"I assume you have news," she said quietly.

"Yes. And it's difficult news." He guided her over to the couch. "The coroner found high levels of potassium in your father's system. That's common with a heart attack."

She nodded, and Mark continued, "But the coroner wasn't convinced. Your father's body was not badly decomposed. Looking at his heart didn't reveal obvious blockage or other signs of heart damage. He was able to find a place on your father's neck where there was a mark. We are fairly certain your father was given the drug potassium chloride. It simulates a heart attack and is lethal in high enough doses." He paused. "We have changed the cause of death for your father from heart attack to homicide." He watched her closely to gauge her reaction.

Her tears started flowing again. How could this have eluded her? She knew how athletic he was and what good care he had taken of himself. She just thought his death was one of those harsh ironies where a lifetime of good habits wasn't enough. And how alone he must have felt. Was he scared? Angry? She had to believe he was indignant about all Reston was doing.

"Thank you," she rasped. "I don't know if anyone else besides you could have put this all together. Really, I'm grateful, even though it will take me a long time to get over this. In my heart, I knew you were right the minute you said it."

"You're the one who identified the clues. You just didn't know they *were* clues. How can I help you?"

"Catch the son of a bitch," she said without blinking.

"That goes without saying. I'm going back into Fargo to work with the police and our unit. I'm concerned about your safety now that we know. Reston may have connections in the Fargo police department. We know he has a connection to the police department in Pelican Rapids. Someone may well have gotten to him and told him we have a warrant out for his arrest. I really think you should come into Fargo and stay there."

She shook her head. "I need to stay here with my pets. I'll be all right. I have the security system now and your gun. I may even be able to shoot it if I need to." The thought of how hard it would be to hit anyone with her adrenaline at full tilt made her almost laugh. She pictured bullets flying in every direction.

"Then I'll come back out here after we get things in motion. Could I stay in one of your empty rooms? I'd feel better not leaving you alone."

"Really, it's unnecessary."

"I'm pretty determined," he mused, not budging.

Walking over to her, he pulled her off her big overstuffed chair, hugged her, and gave her a kiss on the forehead. "You've been really strong through all of this, but you shouldn't be alone now."

Secretly, Carley was relieved. All that had happened had taken a toll. She felt exhausted, physically and emotionally.

"I'll be back around 7:00 tonight. If you don't have any food in the house, we'll order pizza. Don't go out today, promise? If anything happens, call me, not the sheriff's office."

46

Carley hardly knew what to do with herself. She didn't want to venture outside because she didn't know what danger might be lurking there. She pulled a jigsaw puzzle out of the game closet and got started assembling a picture of multicolored dice. After an hour, it made her eyes cross. Abandoning the puzzle, she picked up a book she had started reading several weeks earlier, but even that couldn't hold her interest. She called Trish, and they talked for a while. She went online and onto Facebook, where she stalked Mac briefly. She had promised herself she wouldn't, but she was just too bored to resist. There they were—the happy couple. Or were they? She realized that in many pictures Mac was facing another direction. Well, time would tell.

By 6:00 p.m., she was getting hungry, and Abigail was getting restless. The dog kept looking at her expectantly. Finally, she went and stood by the door, giving out two short barks, the signal it was time for a break. Carley looked outside through the kitchen window and, seeing no activity, let her out. She hoped Abigail didn't decide to chase a squirrel today; Carley wasn't going to leave the house.

A few minutes later, the familiar scratch at the back door announced Abigail was ready to come back in. When Carley opened the door, filling the door frame was Gordon/James holding Abigail Rose tightly and a gun. He grinned his charming, dimpled grin and asked, "Can I come in? I'd like you to hear my side of the story."

Quickly, she tried to shut the door, but he was too fast for her. Inserting his shoe between the door and the doorframe, he pushed with all his strength, nearly knocking her over. All she could think of was where had she set Mark's gun down. *Why isn't it on me?* She glanced around the room, but he said, "Please don't try anything stupid. I've grown attached to this little mutt, and I know you have too. I'd hate to see anything happen to her." Abigail looked up at him unknowingly and licked his chin.

"What do you want from me?" she asked.

"I want you. I want you to come with me. We can get away from all of this. I know a lot of people. And I have a lot of cash stashed away. The Canadian border is only four hours from here. Once we've crossed over, we can go anywhere, and no one will find us. Someplace remote. There are parts of Canada where no one would ever think to look for us. Or we could go someplace exotic like Fiji. Or Bora-Bora."

Ohmygod, Carley thought. *He is crazy. He thinks I'll go with him. And where the hell is Mark? How long until he gets here? How can I stall him?* "Well, I'd better go pack, then. It won't take me long. I need warm clothes if we're heading north. I don't think my passport is good anymore, though. I'll check."

"Don't worry about that. We'll go in through some rough country at night on foot. I already have a car up there. And you'll be with me. Since we'll have cash, you won't even need your credit cards. We'll buy what you need once we're up there. Just come with me now."

"I can't just upend my life like that, especially after you lied to me about who you are. What do I call you, by the way—James or Gordon?"

"Move it, now," he said threateningly.

Carley knew the last thing she wanted to do was go with him, but she didn't think she could stall him for an hour or two until

Mark arrived. Her cell phone was on the other side of the room. She felt completely trapped.

"Tell you what. Put Abigail down and I'll go with you."

"No way. She's my insurance policy."

"You do anything to hurt her and we're finished. Is that what you want? I would never forgive you. We had something—but how do I know I can trust you? Leave Abigail as a first step. Come on. We've had a connection. We can have something special again. Put her down and I'll leave with you. But you must do it now. We're at risk. Everyone is looking for you."

He knew she was right. Hesitating only slightly, he put Abigail close to the floor, and she jumped out of his arms. Carley breathed a sigh of relief. Okay. At least Abigail would be safe. "I have to go to the bathroom. You have to give me that."

He nodded, but first he checked the bathroom to make sure there wasn't an escape window. There wasn't. The window was up high, and she wouldn't fit through it. "Where's your cell phone?"

She pointed to the end table next to the big, overstuffed chair.

"Good. Well, don't just stand there. Get going."

When she came out, she shut the door and put on a brave smile. "Let's go."

Walking out the back door, she saw a gray Chevy Malibu parked in the driveway. No one would be looking for that car. She felt as if she were entering a cave and a big rock was about to block the only way out.

47

They'd only been gone a few minutes when Mark Dolan was knocking on Carley's door. "Come on, come on," he mumbled nervously. There was no answer. He tried the doorknob to see if it was locked, and it wasn't. Abigail, recognizing him, ran around excitedly. "Where is she, girl?"

He entered the house with trepidation, his gun drawn. No one was home, but he knew Carley had no intention of leaving, and he was certain she would have called him if she had changed her mind. He went from room to room, making sure she really wasn't there. Spotting her cell phone and his gun, he knew she was in trouble. What had happened to her? She wasn't in her loft bedroom or either of the downstairs bedrooms. He checked the closets, and nothing was amiss there. He came to the bathroom door, which was closed. He knocked twice, just to be on the safe side, then entered. There were two letters written in lipstick on the mirror: *JR* and the word *Canada*. A jolt went through Mark. Her message had come through loud and clear. In minutes, there was a bulletin out to all law enforcement with a description of Carley, Reston, and his Maserati, though Mark wasn't certain he'd be driving that flashy car if he were smart. Could he intercept them before anything else happened? God, he hoped so.

Meanwhile, Carley was wondering what it would be like to jump out of the car while James was driving eighty miles an hour on these back roads. *Where are radar traps when you need them?* she wondered. No, she liked her skin way too much to jump. She needed a plan for what she might do if they stopped for gas or a bathroom break. Eventually, they would have to stop, wouldn't they? She just didn't want it to be in the middle of nowhere.

James was relaxed, drumming his fingers on the steering wheel. He looked at her and smiled. "What a life we can have. We can live anywhere. I have plenty of money stashed away. We'll figure it out. We're good together, you know."

She smiled. "So, what's your plan? I'm sure you have one. When you have a big prize in mind, you don't seem to stop at anything to get it."

He beamed, then looked at her more closely to see if she was mocking him. He couldn't tell, so he assumed she wasn't. Of course, he was mistaken. "You'll see. It will be awesome."

"I really want to know. Where are we going?" Carley asked.

"Once we cross the border, we'll have a bit of a hike to get to my car that I keep up there. It'll take a few hours, but eventually we'll make our way to Winnipeg. Tomorrow, we'll head to Prince Albert. I have a cabin on a remote lake up there. Used to use it for a fishing getaway. It's nothing fancy, but no one will look for us there."

"Won't the police be able to find out you have property up there?"

"Oh, sweetheart, the property isn't in my name. You don't have to worry your pretty head about that."

She wondered whose name the property was in. How many aliases did he have? Were there other people involved behind the scenes? Or was it just James masterminding the entire plot? Was he smart enough to pull that off?

"How about stopping up ahead?" Carley suggested when she saw freeway signs advertising food. They were approaching the city limits of Grand Forks. "I'm famished. It's way past dinner-time, and I haven't eaten since breakfast. Plus, I need to make a pit stop." She smiled disarmingly.

"It's only been a couple of hours since we left your place. Really? You have to go again? Is there something wrong with you?" he asked menacingly.

"No, I just have to go. I was drinking coffee all afternoon. You can come with me and stand outside the door if you're really worried."

"Oh, I will."

48

Inside the bathroom stall, Carley took out the lipstick and quickly wrote a message on the back of the door. Flushing the toilet, she ran water as if to wash her hands. Outside the restroom, her kidnapper was waiting for her. Wrapping his arm tightly around her shoulder, he pushed her through the busy crowd. She doubted he would shoot her if she screamed, but he might shoot other people who were witnesses. He was infatuated with her, it was clear. Or maybe she was the way James would get ultimate revenge on her father.

* * *

As he sped toward Fargo, Mark was frantically issuing an all-points bulletin alerting police and state highway patrol in both Minnesota and North Dakota. I-29 was the fastest route to Canada, but Reston might suspect there would be a search under way for him. His car would be very conspicuous, if he were driving his own. If he wasn't, tracking him would be exceptionally more challenging. They had tracers on his cell phone, which hadn't been used in hours. It was likely he had a couple of untraceable ones. This could be like trying to find a prairie dog in North Dakota. He jumped in his car, continuing to lay plans through the FBI dispatcher. Fargo had a crack team in place, thanks to the drug trafficking. He'd have a lot of help if he needed it.

Carley and James ate their meal in the parking lot of the fast-food restaurant. It was too cumbersome to manage driving with a stick shift and eating fast food. Carley was grateful for a little time to pass. Hopefully, someone would see her message. She ate as slowly as she could, but James was antsy to get going.

As they drove along, Carley studied Reston's mood carefully. "Don't you think they'll be looking for us?"

"Oh, sure. But by the time they figure out you're gone, they won't have a clue which direction to look."

She was afraid he was right. Would Mark find her message? If he did, would he understand it? That was her only hope right now. Otherwise, they might not find her until it was too late.

"How much longer until we reach the Canadian border?" Carley asked.

"About another hour and a half or so," James responded. "Of course, we're not going all the way to the border. We'll have to ditch this car."

Carley wondered to herself just how many cars he had.

It was now close to 9:00 p.m. The sun didn't set until 9:30 or 10:00; Carley couldn't remember exactly. At least they'd have some light as they drove along. Carley pretended to sleep so she didn't have to talk with James, but she didn't want to lose track of where they were on I-29.

Meanwhile, a small blonde girl in a restroom stall called out, "Mommy, Mommy, look. Someone wrote all over this door."

Glancing at it quickly, the mother steered her daughter away from the writing and said, "You know that's a very bad thing to do, right? You must never ever destroy private property like that."

"I know, Mommy. But look! The person who wrote it wants us to call the police."

Her mother went back into the stall and muttered, "Oh my gosh." She went out to the gas station clerk and said, "There's something in here you've got to see."

Mark took the call with the message. He was right about their direction. And James had changed vehicles, just as he had suspected he would. Taking the light flasher out of his glove compartment, he affixed it to the roof of his car. They had to get to her before they reached the border, or they might not reach her in time. She could be swallowed up by Canadian hinterland.

49

It had been about an hour since their last stop, and Carley wasn't sure Reston would let her stop again, but she had to try.

"Sorry, that large Diet Coke is going right through me."

"Too bad. I'm not stopping again until we're closer to the border. If you have to pee, I'll get off the road and you can pee in a ditch. There's no one out here at this time of night."

"Oh, *please*. You can trust me. I haven't done anything wrong, have I? I want to go with you. I just don't want to get eaten alive by mosquitoes."

He knew she was right. The sunlight was fading, and mosquitoes up here were fierce this time of day. "All right, but no funny business. If I find you're trying to contact anyone, I'll kill you. You know that."

"You can trust me. I don't have anything on me. Look for yourself. None of the restrooms have a window."

Reluctantly, he pulled the car off the freeway. "This is the last time. Get control of your bladder," he told her.

In the gas station, he inspected the stall. No one inside, no way out. "Make it fast."

This time, she really needed to go. Quickly, she sprawled a message on the back of the door with the small tube of lipstick she had smuggled under her bra. God, she hoped someone found it. And believed it.

Reston was leaning up against the side of the wall as she opened the door. "What took you so long?" he growled.

"Really, you want a full accounting?" she responded cockily. With that, she grabbed his hand as if they were a normal couple on their hundredth date. "You know, I'm getting kind of used to the idea of being with you. You don't need to doubt me so much. I know my dad brought us together, so you can't be all bad," she teased.

He looked at her coolly and steered her to the door.

As they neared the door of the gas station, Carley caught a glimpse of a police car almost out of her line of sight that was blocking traffic from entering the parking lot. Immediately, she felt her knees go weak. They were here. But what next? She was terrified there would be a shootout. After all, James had his hand on the gun in his pocket and a tight grip on her. How could she keep him from spotting them?

"Look at this," Carley pointed to a bug spray display, maneuvering James so his back was to the door. "Did you bring any? If you didn't, let's get some. The hike in is going to be miserable. You know I'm right! And they sell windbreakers. I need something to cover my arms. Please." She looked at him pleadingly.

"I have a jacket in the car you can use. Now let's get going," James snarled.

Quickly, she turned to him, gazing into his eyes, and said, "Really? You're going to bite my head off while I'm telling you you don't have anything to worry about? I've wanted you from the first time we met. Now you have me."

He looked her in the eye questioningly, trying to assess her sincerity.

"I mean it. Remember the fun we had kayaking? The fun we had in my bedroom?"

They were nearing the door. She pulled him close to her and gave him a kiss. The last thing she wanted was for him to see what was going on outside.

"Well, I'm glad you've finally come to your senses," James replied as he pulled himself from the embrace and opened the door to go outside.

As he stepped across the threshold, Carley stuck out her foot and tripped him.

His large frame went reeling onto the concrete surface. Three waiting police officers pounced on him, holding him on the ground, forcing his hands behind his back, removing the threat of his gun.

Mark grabbed Carley and pulled her away from the struggling figure, hugging her tightly. "It's over. I've got you."

She nodded and began shaking violently, collapsing in his arms.

"You found me!" she wailed. "I didn't know if you'd see the notes. Or if you'd understand them."

Mark chuckled. "Very smart. We had helpful people all the way up here. It's that good North Dakota spirit," he said with a heartfelt smile.

"Thank you," she whispered.

50

Carley awoke the next morning with a startle. Abigail had jumped onto the bed and was licking her face. "Bad, bad doggy," Carley laughed. She put on her bathrobe, made a cup of coffee, and sat out on the deck overlooking the lake.

She felt like she had been run over by a truck. What a bizarre series of events she had just lived through. She had come to the lake hoping to escape the stress in her life. Instead, she found herself in the middle of a swirl second to none. And now it was over. At least she hoped it was. It would take her a long time to get over what had happened to her dad, but at least she knew what really happened. She had been so completely clueless, which was exactly the way Gordon—or James, really—had wanted her to be. He was pulling strings behind everything that had gone wrong, and she thought she was falling in love with him. It would take a long time before she trusted her judgment about men again. She was wrong about Mac, and she was wrong about Gordon. In a surprisingly nice way, she had been wrong about Mark Dolan too. *Very, very wrong about him*, she thought, smiling.

Mark had been amazing. When he had learned from her restroom jotting that the Maserati had been replaced by a Malibu, he had notified every law enforcement, gas station, and rest stop throughout western Minnesota and eastern North Dakota. The car had been picked up on radar about fifteen minutes from their final stop, not far from the border. She shuddered when she thought how things might have gone down. She owed her life to Mark.

Carley spent the next two days giving statements at the FBI headquarters. The phone had rung off the hook with reporters and friends who had heard about all that had transpired. Joe and Jean called to express their concern for all the trouble she had been through and asked what they could do to help. Jean immediately came over with another batch of blueberry muffins. Trish called to tell her the news had reached the Twin Cities. Mac called to see if she was okay. He asked her if she wanted him to come up to keep her safe. She informed him she felt safer without him in the vicinity. She just wanted to get away from it all and forget about the entire, sordid mess.

Thinking about what lay ahead, suddenly a slow smile crept across her face. She had almost forgotten. Tonight. Jeff. Totally unsuspecting, nice, fun, attentive Jeff. They were going to a movie in Detroit Lakes. A romantic comedy, she recalled. And having hamburgers at the little gourmet burger place. Just what she needed in her life right now. A simple, uncomplicated man with no strings attached. Or had she misjudged him too?

Could she ever relax here again? She hoped so. She knew it would take time. And good friends. But she hoped that Pelican Lake would, at last, be the salve she needed to heal.

Meanwhile, the man three cottages down watched her through his binoculars.

ACKNOWLEDGMENTS

I dedicate this book to my mother, Sunny Mathison, in honor of her hundredth birthday on June 10, 2018, and for the love and support she has unconditionally given.

This book is also dedicated to:
- My daughters, Jill and Laura, for inspiring and encouraging my creativity.
- My sisters, Marcia and Marilyn, for their generous input.
- Murder mystery author Mary Logue for her thoughtful review.
- Eric Larson for his research on homemade bombs.
- Joanne Cavallaro, professor of English at St. Catherine University, for her enthusiastic writing support.
- Rich Sherry for his strategic input.
- Officer Ann Buck and Sergeant Darin Hill of the Hopkins Police Department for contributing reality to police scenes.
- Tom Hembree for his advice on spectrometer innovation.
- Everyone else who has supported me along this journey.